lead him not into temptation

M.L. STEINBRUNN

Interior Design by Jovana Shirley, Unforeseen Editing,
www.unforeseenediting.com
Cover Design by Arijana Karcic, Cover it Designs
Editing by Hot Tree Editing

Printed in the United States of America

First Printing, 2014

ISBN-13: 978-0692279168

Dedication

For my daughters, Ashlynn and Ella. May you always value the gifts you can offer this world. Find strength in yourselves in order to provide kindness and comfort to others. I am proud of who you are and look forward to who you two will become.

With all my love,

Mom

Contents

About the Author vii

Acknowledgements...ix

Prologue 1

Chapter 1 7

Chapter 2..13

Chapter 3..21

Chapter 4..27

Chapter 5..37

Chapter 6..45

Chapter 7..53

Chapter 8..59

Chapter 9..67

Chapter 10..79

Chapter 11..93

Chapter 12..103

Chapter 13..111

Chapter 14..121

Chapter 15..127

Chapter 16..133

Chapter 17..137

Chapter 18..141

Chapter 19..147

Chapter 20..159

Chapter 21..171

About The Author

Colorado native M.L. Steinbrunn is new to the literary community, but has been in love with the world of fictional characters and plot twists since she was a child. Writing short stories and reading anything she could get her hands on, it could be argued that her hobby borders on an obsession.

She works full-time as a middle school and high school educator and coach in rural Colorado where she and her husband are raising their four young children. Through education she has enjoyed guiding others on their paths and helping students build their stories.

In her free time M.L. enjoys travelling, one-clicking books, watching movies, chauffeuring her children to their one and half million activities, and people watching.

She would like to add a big thank you to everyone that has been overwhelmingly supportive of this incredibly scary and exciting journey.

Where to follow her....

Facebook: www.facebook.com/mlsteinbrunn

Twitter: http://twitter.com/MSteinbrunn

Acknowledgements

There are so many people that have helped to make this book possible, I appreciate you all.

My Family: I think they thought that once book one was published, I would have the bug out of my system and I would pack away the laptop. When my husband realized, the bug wasn't going to go away, he surprised me with a new, smaller computer to keep the series going. He and my children have been extremely understanding, and that has meant so much. Thank you, you guys. This book has a special place in my heart, as I was writing pages the night that my youngest son was born and just days later once we were released from the hospital.

My Hometown: My hometown community fully embraced my first book and has been patiently waiting for this book to release. Almost everyone I know, picked up a copy of Forgive Us Our Trespasses, even if they had no intention of reading it, just to show their support for me. Even knowing that these books are romance novels, my tiny, conservative community has supported this endeavor and has encouraged me every step of the way. I truly appreciate that support.

Indie Author/Blogger Community: I have found this online literary community to be one of the most inspiring and compassionate groups. There have been so many authors and blogs that stepped up to help me, talk me off the ledge, donate, and share announcements. I appreciate every one of you. Ladies of the Indies Round Table and Indie Erogenous Zone, thank you so much for being there for me. You are the best! My Magnificent Minions, you ladies are absolutely wonderful. You are more than a street team; you guys are a group of friends that have provided a tremendous amount of support. Thank you, girlies. There are several individuals that had a major hand in this project and deserve a special thank you. Becky, Jennifer, and all of the betas at Hot Tree Editing, this team made this a story worth reading. My beta team: Natalie, Jen, Jenna, Con, Alicia, Missy, Shauna, Silla, and Ashlee, thank you so much for taking the time to read this book and offering valuable, honest feedback. Your comments and opinions truly made this book so much better. Ari with Cover it Designs thank you for my gorgeous cover. Jovana at Unforeseen Editing did the formatting for this book and made it something beautiful. All of the blog tours and release blitz events were organized by Ena and Jennifer at Enticing Journey Promotions. You ladies did a wonderful job, and I appreciate all of your hard work. Thank you to all of the blogs and authors that participated in the release of this book. It found its way into the hands of readers because of you.

Readers: Thank you all so much for taking a chance on me and this series. None of my efforts would have mattered if I didn't have your support. Thank you so much for allowing me the opportunity to follow this dream.

Prologue

JEN

"Does Dad know?" I ask, staring blankly out the window reluctant to make eye contact with my mother in the driver's seat. She takes a deep breath, maintaining her sights on the road ahead. Apparently, she can't look at me either.

"He knows," she whispers, before clearing her throat with the words, which seem to be strangling her. "I called him as soon as we knew, so he could start making arrangements. He is waiting for us to arrive home."

I don't respond. There is nothing to say. I can't explain to them what happened to me and my father will be unforgiving no matter the situation. All that is left to do is to keep my head down and wait for the hammer of my father to fall. I continue to keep my eyes on the grid pattern of the city streets out my passenger window, letting it pull me into a daze as I attempt to escape my impending reality.

I become entirely engulfed in my daydream, one which includes starting and finishing my senior year of high school with the friends I thought I had, with a guy I thought cared about me. I was so wrong. I don't even notice when my mother pulls into the driveway of our massive colonial home. It's an impressive sight to behold. To me it's just my home, but to my parents it has always been more important what this house said to the public. It certainly makes a statement. It screams money; the front pillars exhibit strength and power, just like the house's inhabitants. My father, Andrew MacLauchlan, master politician, wouldn't have it any other way.

It's not until I hear the driver's side door slam when I realize we've parked. My mother walks to the front of our car and waits for me to vacate the car and follow her into the house. I have no choice but to unbuckle my seatbelt, the only thing that is providing any security at the moment, and head toward my waiting parents.

I walk slowly behind my mother, the cement driveway clicking under her designer shoes, while my summer sandals squeak against my sweaty feet. She opens the front door, but I remain still in the entryway as she delicately places her keys and purse on the curio table. I feel frozen in place. My stomach is churning, my hands are clammy, and I feel like I could pass out from the fear of what awaits me on the other side of the door. I want to run up the stairs to my room and avoid the inevitable conversation, maybe run back to the car and leave for good. Before I can allow my feet to move me in either direction, my father's voice breaks my train of thought.

"Jennifer, please meet me in my office," my father's voice echoes down the hallway. The tone is stern but not loud, which only sends my already quivering nerves into overdrive. Yelling would signal his anger, even disappointment, but a silent, angry version of my father is ferocious. He is in lion mode, ready to pounce and destroy. It's what has made him the best lawyer in Denver and now, a star politician in the Colorado State Senate who is currently facing reelection. He is a man to be reckoned with, and he is about to handle me.

I push my blonde, curly hair away from my face, noticing the beads of sweat, which have gathered along my hairline, square my shoulders, and glide toward the door to the office. I pause before taking the cool door handle into my hand. I take a deep breath, and slowly creaks open the heavy office door to see my father standing behind his large mahogany desk. I'm thankful his back is to me and his attention is focused on the papers he's shuffling through; I don't think I'm ready to see what he thinks of me. Instead of entering the room completely I stand, waiting for instruction. There will be instruction, there always is. I am never in control of household conversations, and this situation is no different.

"Take a seat, Jennifer," he says in a low, smooth tone, which is more scary than comforting. I do as I'm told, sliding onto the couch, letting the cool feel of the leather temporarily calm my flushed skin. I keep my head down, staring at the expensive Persian rug under my feet. I feel the tears begin to burn my eyes, but I push them back in an attempt to hold my emotions together. My mother enters the room and closes the door behind her. Apparently, my social climbing mother has decided I'm worth more than an accessory and my actions have impacted her status at the country club. Her presence merely indicates she needs to know how to proceed in order to maintain her place with the ladies who lunch.

I take a deep breath, gathering the strength to defend myself and explain as best I can. I have no memory of the evening, only the end result of the events, which occurred. My father is the least understanding person I know. I can only hope he will show me at least a slight bit of compassion.

"I know you think I've been careless. I can only imagine what this will do to the upcoming campaign, but Daddy, please believe me. I had no idea." I exhale the ragged breath vibrating in my throat from fear. I scoot closer to the edge of the couch in an attempt to further plead my case. "I was at a party, a few weeks ago. Preston Lexington had finally asked me out and we went together. He acted like such a gentleman, offering to get my drinks all evening, even though I only drank soda. Amber hung

3

out with us for part of the night and we had a good time listening to the band that was invited to play. But then…"

"Enough," he interrupts, almost sighing the word as if my story is hurting him.

"But Daddy, let me explain," I beg, the lump in my throat becoming unbearable. "I woke up in my car the next morning with tattered clothes and no memory of most of the night after arriving at the party. Preston was gone, Amber was gone; I was alone in the driveway with no idea of how I got there." The tears roll down my cheeks and I choke on the words I'm trying desperately to spill out. My mother just listens, and my father hasn't even turned to look at me. My pleas are falling on deaf ears. "Please, Daddy, believe me," I whisper.

"Believe you?" he bellows, turning swiftly to challenge my request. "It doesn't matter what I believe, it doesn't matter what really happened. They only thing which matters is what we can prove, what we can make other people believe."

He throws the documents he was clutching onto the coffee table in front of me; the pictures spilling across the slick varnished top. I hear my mother gasp at the sight before her. I can barely see the images through my tears, but I recognize enough to know nothing I say will ever matter. I've ruined us. The churning in my stomach takes over as I rush to the trashcan and empty the little bit of food I have in my stomach. Once my body has stopped shaking and the nauseous wave passes, I take a tissue from my father's desk and return to my seat.

"I didn't do this, I don't remember doing any of this," I stutter.

"Stop. Just stop it. This is an election year; do you realize how damaging this is? Even if the pictures were our only issue here, this could ruin us," he snaps. "I've done what I could to contain everything, but you can't be here right now. I've arranged for you to stay with your Aunt Margaret in Montana for your senior year; she will homeschool you. I plan to tell everyone you are caring for your sick aunt, which will help to explain the doctor's appointments."

He states everything so matter-of-factly; my feelings are completely disregarded. "You can't just send me away, I can't disappear like that, Dad. I can't just disappear."

"Yes I can, Jennifer, and yes you will. This disaster is beyond my imagination. It will take a great deal of money, favors, and God knows what else to clean it up. You being here, in the state you're in will only make it worse. When everything is done, your mother will take you to college in Fort Collins. Your bags are already packed and your flight is in a few hours. I suggest you let the friends you thought you had, know you're leaving to care for your ailing aunt and that you won't be able to contact them once you've arrived. I've arranged for your Aunt Margaret to have temporary guardianship of you while staying with her. All arrangements have been made."

"Andrew, what about these pictures? We can't just hide these. The wives will surely catch wind of them; we will be social pariahs." Of course, my mother is only thinking of herself. She, too, could care less about me, her daughter, her only child. She has no concern for the assault, which I have no recollection of, or consequences of the horrific event for me. Her primary concern is where this will land her within her social circles.

"These are the only remaining copies, Kim," he says, taking a seat behind his desk while looking at documents laid out in front of him. He is finished with this conversation, not even bothering to look at us as he speaks. "It took a little legal muscle, but we have the photos. All other copies and negatives have been destroyed. Soon these will be too."

Bracing myself, I grip onto the arm of the couch and pull myself up to stand before my father. I wipe the mess of snot and tears from my face and address my father one last time. Gathering every bit of courage I have, I finally speak the words I need to say to these people who claim to be my parents.

"I hope one day the two of you learn to love something more than just yourselves, more than power, or social status. I hope one day, you figure out how to protect the people you should love, and hopefully I still care enough to want that love."

Before they can respond, I turn and leave the room, walking away from the life I knew and the friends and family I never really had.

Spring 2014

JEN

"What in the hell?" I croak out, pulling the cocoon of blankets off my head and slightly cracking open one eye to see the sun is barely peeking through the curtains. I reach for my nightstand to find the source of my uninvited morning wakeup call...Campbell. After sliding my finger across the answer bar, I snuggle back down into my warm haven, to find out what in the hell has her panties in a twist.

"Cam, there better be a good reason for this phone call before the hour of butt crack. The normal population is not up right now," I say, ending my rant with a yawn to emphasize my point.

"The hour of butt crack?" she chuckles. "As in the butt crack of dawn?"

"Exactly. It's early, Campbell. Why are you calling me? We have a shoot today and I need my beauty sleep to make the magic happen."

"You definitely can make magic happen," rasps the smooth, baritone voice from the other side of my bed. Shit! My eyes widen at the realization he is still here and I turn quickly to cover his mouth with my hand to silence him. I use the word he, well, because I'm sure he has a name, yet it escapes me at the moment. I hear Campbell speaking on the other end, but my attention is focused on the groping hands and warm body moving closer to me.

"Hello? Jen? Did you flipping fall asleep? Wake up, Jen!" Campbell shouts, forcing me to pull the phone away from my ear.

"Yes, sorry. You got me. I fell asleep. What was that again?" I ask. Campbell doesn't need to know my lack of attention is because the model from yesterday's photo shoot didn't get the memo that I don't do sleepovers. Sex, yes. On my terms, absolutely, but never snuggly sleepovers.

"Jesus, Jen, it's like seven in the morning. The waking world is in fact moving around at this hour. Anyways, we had to change the time of the photo shoot. They're calling for rain this afternoon, so we're moving everything up to this morning. I'm calling you to get your ass up and moving so we can meet up with the band at ten."

"All right, then, got it. See you there. Thanks, Cam." I hang up on her before she utters another word and I jump out of bed, swatting grabby hands away, and covering myself with the sheets.

"Thanks for the sex and all, but my schedule has changed and I need to get going for the day," I tell Brad, Bryan, Braxton…I'm almost positive it's a 'B' name.

"Well, let me get your day off on the right start, baby," he coos, grabbing ahold of my sheet and pulling me closer to him.

I rip the sheets from his hands and walk toward his clothes piled up on the floor near the doorway. "Um, thanks but I'm good," I say, gathering up his clothes and throwing them at him. "If I need your assistance in the future, I'll be sure to save your number."

The stunned look on his face is almost priceless. He is absolutely gorgeous and surprisingly not bad in bed either. I'm sure this is the first time he's been kicked out of a woman's bed. In fact, I would bet I'm stealing lines out of his dating playbook. However, repeat sexual encounters are not my thing. I always assume control of a situation and never a let a man too close. If anyone is going to walk away hurt, it's going to be him. They always say it's a man's world, and in regards to my sex life, I have no problem wearing the pants and playing the dickhead role.

"You have got to be kidding me? You're telling me to leave?" he asks, while roughly putting on his wrinkled clothes. Reason two why I always invite men to my house instead of venturing in their dirty habitats; I will never do a wrinkled walk of shame. No, thank you.

"Look…" I let the word hang in the air waiting for him to fill me in on his less than memorable name.

"Cooper."

I grimace. "Damn, I was way off," I say shaking my head, and then lead him into the living room. "The only reason you are still here is because I fell asleep last night before I could show you the door. I'm sure I'll see you around and if the moment strikes us, maybe we can have round two. We both had a good time, let's not ruin it by having some awkward morning-after exchange."

I've left the poor guy speechless. He follows me to the door, which I open for him. He swoops down and picks up his shoes he left in the entry and steps into the hall. He's still looking at me, which surprises me, usually men get the spiel, are relieved they didn't have to deliver the lines, and leave with a smile. Cooper, not so much.

"You're a bitch, you know that right? Women don't act like this. Women don't treat men like me, like this."

I won't lie, his words sting a little, but they are entirely true. I am a bitch, for good reason, and I will never apologize for it. "You're right. I am a bitch, but you know what? I am a smart bitch who can play a man's game. The only reason you're pissed is because I took the words out of your mouth and left you with morning wood. Now, I'll see ya around, Coop."

I slam the door in his face, drop my sheet, and walk to the bathroom for a much-needed shower. Not only do I need to wash that little prick Cooper off me, but I need to gear up for a photo shoot which I have no doubt will test every bit of patience I don't have. I've only met the guys from Absolution once and I'm not too pleased to have any more dealings with them. Their lead singer is the epitome of douche lead singer who is only in the music industry because of the pussy it can land him. Their drummer is a big, teddy bear who sweats like he walks around in a sauna all day, not exactly great material for a photographer. Their bassist, well, I didn't talk to him, so I can't criticize...yet. Then there is their lead guitar player, Casen. He's infuriating with how he tries to be all insightful all the time. Which is code for I think he likes to hear himself talk and I would like nothing more than to gag him with their drummer's tube sock. I mean that in the least sexual way possible.

Damn, I need to remember to stop at Starbucks on the way, or I may end up making one of them a tripod Popsicle, or worse, end up in bed with another Cooper.

Between showering, finding the right outfit, checking emails, and surfing my regular social media sites, I step into a coffee shop with only twenty minutes until ten and am met with the longest line imaginable. FUCK! I have two options and I pull out my phone to let Campbell decide between the two.

> *Me: Stuck in an ungodly line at Starbucks. MUST have coffee to survive. Two options...I will be late but caffeine will help me play nice. Or I'm on time and you get me coffee so I play nice.*

> *Campbell: Damn it, Jen!!*

> *Me: PLEASE!!!*

> *Campbell: You're lucky I love you. I'll get your coffee. Get your ass here.*

> *Me: Thank you! See you in twenty!*

lead him not into temptation

I run out of the coffee shop and race downtown to the Civic Center Park. Downtown Denver is always a mess; the one-way streets and meter parking is a nightmare. I finally find a place to park with minutes to spare; of course, the band is already set up and Campbell is standing at the fountain with my coffee in hand, waiting for me.

"I know, I know. I'm lucky you love me," I say as I snatch the vanilla latte from her hand and drink the first and best sip of the liquid gold.

CASEN

"I know, I know. I'm lucky you love me," I hear her tell Campbell as she takes the coffee from her and guzzles it like it's a bottle of water and not a cup of hot coffee.

I've only met Jen once, but the girl is hard to forget. Spitfire is how I would describe her…and talented. Photographers are a dime a dozen, but if you want a good photographer who can, with a click of her camera, land your band on the cover of Rolling Stone, well Jen MacLauchlan is who you call. When I found out our publicist/manager, Campbell, was friends with her, of course we asked that she hire Jen.

To say we didn't hit it off the first time we met is putting it mildly. She is a man-eating firecracker who has no problem putting men in their place, and she did exactly that with me. I would like nothing more than to repay the favor. Her reputation certainly precedes her, but I didn't need to hear the rumors or stories to know what kind of woman Jen MacLauchlan is. She is a dainty little thing who can gobble up a man with one small smile, then cut him to the quick with a quip, which stings like a whip. You do not fuck with women like Jen, but I found it pretty damn fun getting her goat and I have no intention of backing off at today's shoot. Am I a pest? Probably. Immature? Maybe a little, but if I can make this high-strung woman squirm, well, then I would call this shoot a success.

"Hey guys, you ready to get started?" she asks, bending down to grab her camera from her camera bag. Her ability to squat in the skin-tight jeans and knee-high boots she's wearing is beyond my imagination, but I'm not going to complain because the view is pretty nice. Her long, blonde, wavy hair freely lands on her bare shoulder which her knit sweater is having trouble covering; also, not a bad view.

"We've been ready for half an hour, sweetheart. Just waitin' on you," I tell her as I lean against the fountain. John, our drummer, gives me a nudge hard enough to almost knock me into the water. "Dude, shush," he whispers harshly at me.

Jen pushes the strands of hair, which have fallen into her face behind her ear, allowing me to see her honey brown eyes slide to my direction and then narrow in on my face. Oh yeah, I've pissed her off. She recovers quickly, trying to remain professional. "Well then, these pictures should be amazing," she says with a tight smile as she stands to walk toward us. Her eyes are glued on me, almost challenging me to make another smartass comment.

"Okay, everyone," Campbell interrupts, clapping her hands. "Let's get going before the rain moves in. Jen, tell them where you want them, and boys, cooperate and get the pictures we need for the tour."

I throw my hands in the air, surrendering to Campbell. After all, the only reason we have the opportunity at this tour is because of her. A major label hasn't picked us up yet, but this statewide mini-tour is absolutely a step in the right direction. Our band, Absolution, has only been together for two years and the dives we've been playing have been, well, sad really. It wasn't until a few months ago when Campbell came into the picture that doors began to open for us, including this tour.

"Just tell me where you want me, doll face," our lead singer Royce announces, snaking his arm around Jen's tiny waist. "I'm at your disposal," he whispers suggestively in her ear. I just roll my eyes; leave it to Royce to hit on our photographer. I may want to give her a little shit to make the day interesting and pay her back for the shit she dished out to me the night I first met her, but Royce takes things to a new level. I'm not even sure he enjoys music; his primary interest is in the quantity of ass the microphone can score him.

Jen takes his arm and moves it off of her with just her index finger and thumb as though she doesn't want to touch him, her face scrunched in disgust. "I appreciate the offer, Roy, is it?"

"Royce," he clarifies smoothly.

"Yes, well, Roy, I have plenty of whatever you're offering at my disposal, and I guarantee, none of those options come with a prescription for gonasyphaherpilaids. So, thanks, but for right now, all I need you to do is get your ass away from mine and by the fountain so I can photograph you."

Royce looks back and forth between Jen and I, trying to figure out his best saving face move, eventually deciding to quietly take a seat on the edge of the fountain next to John.

"Anyone else have anything they want to say, or can I do my job now?" Jen asks, her arms squarely folded across her chest. We all shake our heads and look down like we've been scolded by our mothers.

"We're sorry for being such pricks, we really are happy you're here to do this for us," John the peacemaker pipes up.

Jen sighs loudly, obviously annoyed with our antics. "It's fine, let's just get this moving along. I would imagine none of us want to have to come back for a do-over if the rain fucks with our shoot."

Immediately she starts directly everyone where to stand and what to do. Royce is eating up every bit of the attention, while John tries to hide behind his drum set; he hates being the center of attention. Our shy bassist, Seiger, yeah, his name is Seiger, he's one of six in his family and they all have unusual names. The best part? His mom and dad are named Rob and Sue. I don't really have much of a family, so his family usually takes us in around the holidays and his little brother, Wolfgang, tags along with us to most of our shows. Anyways, he acts clueless most of the time, I'm surprised he realizes we are even at the park taking pictures. Don't get me wrong, he's the nicest guy, but man is he in his own world. Me? I feel so uncomfortable with the whole thing. I completely understand the nature of the beast and how publicity, photo shoots, and fans all get rolled into the ball of wax, which is the music machine. Really though, I would like nothing more than to write and play music without all the rest of it. I don't need the famous status, like Royce; I don't care about my name being splashed everywhere and all the girls it can get me. All I want is enough money to keep doing what I love. And in terms of girls, of course I'm a guy who likes a little play now and then, but I'd be happy with one awesome girl and a family of my own.

"I think we have it, boys," Jen announces after what feels like hours of posing and pretending to play my guitar. Thank God. As we start to put our instruments away, the clouds open up and the rain begins to pound down on us. I quickly scramble to put my guitar in its case. I might kill someone if it gets ruined. For a long time it was the only thing of value I owned. When I turned eighteen and left my grandmother's it was the only thing I had with me. I don't care if I have a million dollars, it will always be the guitar, which means the most to me.

I catch Jen continuing to take pictures of us, ignoring the rain pelting her delicate skin. Her hair is beginning to stick to her head, all waves now turning into a dripping mess. Her mascara she obviously spent an immense amount of time applying to perfection is now running down her face. I take a look around at the images she is attempting to freeze in time, and I'm impressed. The guys have secured their instruments and are drenched, splashing in the fountain. The pictures she's taking now will no doubt be the ones, which will end up on our publicity flyers. After all the shit I attempted to throw at her throughout the shoot, now I feel like a bit of a dick for making the day rough on her. Here she is sticking it out in the rain to make our dumbasses look like rock gods. I should be thanking her, not giving her grief.

I try to hang back and enjoy the moment until Jen officially finishes by putting her camera in her camera bag. Then I lunge for her, lifting her into the air, and throwing her into the fountain. John follows my lead and grabs Campbell to do the same.

Campbell comes up laughing, wiping her ebony hair from her face. "Jen is going to give you a lobotomy with her tripod, Casen. You are aware of that, right?" she giggles. Well, shit. So much for lightening the mood and having some fun after a tense day.

"You asshole!" Jen gargles as she shoots to the water's surface. "Do you have any idea how much these boots cost? They are ruined!" Queen bitch on wheels has returned and I'm back on the radar.

Great, just when I think I could maybe play around with princess sparkplug, I step into a massive pile of flaming dog shit. "Sorry, Jen, really. I just thought we could have a little fun. I don't think we got off on the right foot and I was trying to remove some of the tension. My bad," I tell her, holding out my hand to help her out of the fountain. Apparently, my schmuck status has now reached an all-time high.

"And throwing my ass in a cold fountain seemed like the right course of action?" she huffs. "Most civilized people just buy someone a drink." She takes my hand and throws her soaked boot onto the side of the fountain to hoist herself up. I move to pull her up, but instead I'm met with resistance. "It's a good thing I'm not always civilized either," she says with a sly smile as she yanks on my arm. I lose my balance and feel myself being pulled into the frigid water.

She and Campbell are laughing hysterically when I come back up for air. "I'm glad you ladies can have some fun at my expense," I say, wiping the water out of my eyes and trudging to the side of the fountain to climb out. "I thought civilized people were above such nonsense."

"I never have a problem stooping a little lower in order for a little payback," Jen laughs as she and Campbell help each other out of the water. They both are beginning to shiver, but are still laughing at the entire situation, which if I must admit, is somewhat comical. My bandmates are certainly finding the scene entertaining.

"I would think for a politician's daughter, you would never venture below your rank," I joke as I peel off my button-down shirt and wring out the T-shirt underneath. "How about we both act civilized and we all go for drinks?"

The cessation of laughter draws my attention away from my shirt and when I look up I'm met with two serious expressions. Jen looks as though she is both stunned and pissed beyond belief. I wouldn't think such a look would be possible, yet Jen is pulling it off like a pro. I look to Campbell for a little assistance on what I did or said which was so wrong, but she only offers a look of disappointment.

"What? What did I say?" I ask confused. I thought we were having a good time, messing around, but I guess I fucked the moment up.

"Nothing, it's fine. Cam and I have a get-together with the girls, so I'll pass on the drink," she quickly says, turning her back to me to start gathering her bags of equipment. Fuck. She's not pissed, I've hurt her feelings. I step toward her to offer an apology, but Campbell stops me.

"Leave it," she whispers when Jen is out of earshot.

I can feel the lines between my brows deepen. I may not be the brightest crayon in the box, but I know when to offer an apology and apparently this moment calls for one; I've offended Jen in some way. While I meant to serve up a decent ration, it was never my intention for her to leave hurt today.

"What do you mean, 'leave it,' Cam? I obviously said something wrong. I should apologize," I explain as I move past her.

Jen has her back to me, hastily throwing her bags over her shoulders. The poor thing looks like a pack mule; I'm honestly surprised she doesn't hire an assistant to lug around all of her equipment. Having her back to me actually makes this uncomfortable task of groveling much more bearable.

"I'm not sure what I said to upset you, but..."

"Don't fucking worry about it. I don't need an apology from someone beneath my rank, remember?" she seethes as she twirls around to face me. Her bags nail me in the gut, knocking the wind out of me, barreling me over to attempt to catch my breath. Before I can say anything, defend myself, offer up a fuck you right back...anything, she storms off in the direction in which she arrived, bags and all.

"I warned you to stay away, Casen," Cam says when she strides up next to me and nudges my shoulder.

"Seriously, Cam, I didn't have a chance to even slightly backtrack. I was dead in the water," I add. "You would have thought I called her a C-you-next-Tuesday, the way she reacted. What in the hell?"

"Case, in Jen world, that's exactly what you called her. Give her a little time to cool down, she'll get over it," she reassures me, taking my button-down from me and giving it a better wringing, like it will make a difference with the constant rain which is pouring on us.

"Face it, dude, you have the worst luck possible," Royce interrupts.

"What the fuck are you talking about?" I ask, feeling myself getting angry about the overall situation.

"Oh, come on, dude. When it comes to women, you have the worst luck ever. It could be raining pussy right now and you would get smacked in the head with a dick."

John and Seiger have joined the group and are bursting into laughter, while Campbell tries to contain her amusement; at least she's polite. It all heightens my irritation.

"Fuck you guys, I'm going home to get dry," I spout off before turning my calmer attention to Campbell. "Cam, let me know when the pictures are ready, please." She agrees and I take off toward my truck. I hope the walk in the rain will wash this horrible fucking day and my tainted mood off. There is no chance it will take away replaying thoughts of Jen soaked through with her camera, before I fucked it all up.

JEN

The photo shoot for Absolution took longer than I wanted it to, but I still had plenty of time to run home and change into some dry clothes before meeting the girls for our weekly coffee outing. Since Vivian moved back to Denver, the four of us always make sure to carve out time each week to get together at A Scone's Throw, our favorite little mom and pop coffee shop.

I should have offered Campbell a ride from the shoot, but Casen Thompson put me in such a tizzy the only thing I could think of was getting the hell out of there. He did nothing the entire day except attempt to piss me off; it was like he wanted to see me angry. He thinks he's God's gift to women, with his shaggy, sandy brown hair, grey eyes, tall, toned body, and three-quarter sleeve tattoos. He's gorgeous, I'll admit that, but he knows it, and that's worse. I hate guys like him, they are only good for one thing, and I already had a Cooper for the week. I tried to be professional, but I wanted nothing more than to rip off his balls and make earrings out of them. I'm positive the fashion trend would take off once I plastered flyers of them all over Denver with a huge headline, which read, 'Casen Thompson is a ball-less prick.'

I take a deep breath, attempting to calm my annoyed self, before pulling open the door to the coffee shop. I love these girls. They are my family and I would do anything for any of them. I don't want my shitty morning to spill into my afternoon girl time.

Cam and Vivian are already at our table when I've finally composed myself enough to enter. "Hello, my chicas," I say, as I plop myself down in my usual chair. Cam has since changed from the photo shoot and looks comfortable in her tattered jeans, sneakers, and Van Morrison T-shirt. Her hair is still wet and piled high in a ponytail. This was her typical attire in college, but now she reserves her cozy clothes for casual days with us. Most other times, she looks like something out of a 1950s pinup magazine. When she sees me, she gives me a slight wave and a tight smile. Yup, she is approaching with caution.

Vivian, on the other hand, is absolute perfection. Two years ago after her husband Will died, I couldn't say the same thing about her, but now her life is one which most would be jealous of. She married Brooks and moved into his colossal cabin. Their kids have blended together like the fucking Brady Bunch, and now she's pregnant. I guess that's what a St. Lucia honeymoon will do for you; I'm glad neither is in my future.

Her smile is big and bright, and her greeting is even warmer. She stands when I reach the table and pulls me into her famous momma bear hug. I pat her back and move to my seat as quickly as possible to order a caramel macchiato. If I were in a better mood, she would have gotten a slap on the ass, like usual.

"Okay, what's wrong?" Viv asks, noticing my less than enthusiastic greeting. "I never get a pitiful tap on the back from you, girly," she adds as she sits back down.

I immediately pick up the menu from the center of the table and nonchalantly flip through it. "What?" I ask casually. "I'm good, just a rough morning dealing with immature musicians, in the rain no less." I slide my eyes over the menu to peer at Campbell across the table. "I don't know where you find these assholes, but really, Cam, it's time to swim in a bigger, better pond."

"Oh whatever, Jen. If that shoot had lasted any longer, you probably would have taken one of them home," she jokes.

"Bite your tongue, woman!" I sneer. "The only one who even seemed half-way decent was their guitarist and he proved himself to be a grade-A fucktard."

The waitress makes her way to the table just as my expletive spills out of my mouth. She places Cam's coffee and Vivian's tea on the table and looks to me disapprovingly for my order. Yes, ma'am, I'm a potty mouth; we've been coming here for months and my language is just as inappropriate on each occasion. I'm not sure why she thinks her scolding expression will change that now.

"Caramel macchiato, please," I tell her, smiling sweetly which only earns me a headshake as she walks away.

"Ohhhh, tell me more about this guitarist. Details, girls." Viv moves to the edge of her chair and leans in on the table. "Hot? Muscles? Tattoos…"

"Asshole," I simply say, cutting off her inquisition.

She looks to Campbell to elaborate, and Cam immediately accommodates, providing a play-by-play of my hideous morning. Vivian listens intently while I sit back and sip the coffee the waitress delivers. When she finally finishes her story, I look to Vivian to begin the musician bashing, but instead I'm met with wide eyes.

"Jen likes a boy, Jen likes a boy!" she shouts, clapping her hands. The outburst causes me to choke on my coffee and burn my tongue. Campbell just nods and smiles.

"I'm sorry, where the fuck did that come from? Did you not hear the story? He was a dick to me."

"Oh, I heard the story," she answers, wiggling her eyebrows. "I heard how you bickered with a tall, hot, tatted guitar player all morning. You usually put them in their place and move on, but here you sit, still steaming over your encounter. So, once again, Jen likes a boy, Jen likes a boy," she sings.

"I'm not fucking twelve, Viv. Get over it."

"I'm not going to disagree," Campbell interjects, laughing at my pure mortification. "I have to ask though, what in the hell is gonasyphaherpilaids?"

Both of my friends look to me for the definition of my new favorite word for assholes who can't keep it in their pants. "Think of the wide spectrum of venereal diseases; now mesh them all together and you have the king hybrid of all the major ones...gona...sypha...herpa...aids. There are just some guys you look at and know, their rotten dicks will give me a buffet of issues which require prescription medication. I like my vajayjay; I try not to anger her."

They are rolling with laughter by the end of my explanation, provoking the attention of nearby patrons and more nasty looks from our waitress. Her twenty-five percent is slowly finding its way back into my pocket...lighten up, lady.

"I certainly don't mean to change the subject because I love any opportunity possible to poke fun at Jen's love life, but has anyone heard from Carly? She should be here by now," Campbell asks, wiping the tears from her eyes.

We all check our phones to make sure we hadn't missed a text or call from her, but we all come up empty. I look back to the front door of the coffee shop when I hear the bell, which hangs from the door, chime. There stands Carly, soaked through, swollen red eyes, and no little Olivia tagging along behind like usual.

"She's here, girls," I say, directing everyone's attention to the entrance. Immediately Vivian stands up to rush toward her, also noticing her distraught state. Carly puts a hand in the air and shakes her head to stop her and then slowly makes her way across the coffee shop to our table. Vivian takes the cue, and sits back down, watching her like a hawk until she, too, takes her seat with us.

Carly is our shy, carefree, loveable corner piece to our little friend puzzle. She is fiercely loyal and wants everyone to get along; to see her so upset, something has definitely turned her world upside down. She would never let us see her this way, and absolutely not in public.

"Honey, what happened?" Cam asks, handing her a napkin to dry herself off. "Where is Olivia?"

"She's with Jack. I told him I was meeting you girls after our doctor's appointment this morning." Her answer is barely audible and her eyes are down, burning a hole into the table top.

"This morning? Sweetie, it's late afternoon. What have you been doing all day if your appointment was this morning?" I ask, as I reach over and place my hand on hers which, are laced in her lap. Vivian takes note and begins to rub her back.

"Walking," she whispers, still refusing to look up at us.

I glance around the table at the others and we all make eye contact, I can feel the concern radiate from them. She has been walking around Denver all day in the rain, alone. "Are you hurt, what happened?" I ask again. I try to be compassionate and not too gruff with her, but my own worry level is spiking.

She finally looks up at me, tears spilling over her lids and down her frozen cheeks. "We can't have any more children," she answers. Her lips tremble from both the cold as well as the pain the words are inflicting on her.

"What do you mean, hun?" Cam asks handing her another napkin. "You had Olivia with no problems, what's changed?"

Accepting the napkin, Carly dabs her cheeks and eyes before taking a deep breath to gather a reply. "The doctor called it secondary infertility. I guess it's more common than you would think. Jack and I have been trying for almost a year to get pregnant again, and nothing. There can be lots of reasons for it and we can try lots of things fertility-wise to get pregnant."

"So there you go," I say, squeezing her hand. "There are still options, it just might be a little more difficult than the first time."

She shakes her head and looks down at the table again. "No," she sighs. "Jack told me after the appointment that he doesn't want to try anything. He's done, and wants us to move on with our lives. Content with how things are."

"What?" I shout. "That is fucked up of him. If he wanted to be ball-less, all he had to do is ask. I'd gladly fuck up his area, one short and curly at a time." Vivian gives me her best stern mother look to get me to settle down. Cam looks around the coffee shop and begins to quietly apologize for my verbal diarrhea.

"I know, right. That is super fucked up," Carly finally announces, just as loudly as my outburst. "I love him, but what an asshole!" she adds. Vivian gasps, Cam's eyes bulge out of her head, and I can't help but laugh. Carly does not cuss…at all. In fact, she hates when anyone around her uses foul language. She looks around the table at the wide array of reactions to her potty mouth slip-up and she too begins to laugh.

As upset as she is, I think a little of the weight of the situation has been lifted with our laughter. These women truly are my sisters. After walking away from my parents and their money, they are the only family I have, other than Aunt Maggie. It hurts me to see one of them hurt, and this situation only highlights that for me. As much as I like Brooks and Jack, if they ever betrayed my girls, I'd be the first one there with a shovel to help hide the body. If Campbell ever settled down and brought a man into our circle, I would offer her the same service. However, as much as I love them, and I know they love me, I've never felt confident enough to tell them the one thing I fear would change everything. Now, after hearing this from Carly, I know I have to bury my secret even further. I can't risk losing them.

CASEN

A few weeks have passed since the photo shoot at the park, and to say I've been patiently waiting on the call telling me the pictures were ready would be a huge lie. I have called to check in with Campbell every other day, hoping she would offer up the good news. I even wrangled Jen's number from Campbell and texted her a few times to say I was sorry for being a dick. Not only did I want to talk to her again and actually apologize, but I was hoping she would tell me the pictures were ready to see.

This morning when Cam called and told me to gather the band and meet at Rock Bottom Brewery to discuss something important, I've never moved so quickly to get my ass somewhere before. I was almost thirty minutes early to the meeting when I arrived at the restaurant. I thought it would be a good idea to get there a little early and have a beer to calm my nerves.

I wasn't expecting to see anyone here yet, so I was more than shocked to see Jen sitting at the bar, drinking a beer and laughing it up with the bartender. I can't seem to make my feet move, instead I'm standing in the entrance, staring at her. The only word which comes to mind as I watch her free, uninhibited moment is divine…her laugh is intoxicating, her hair is shiny and gorgeous, and her tiny little body looks even smaller in the oversized barstool she's sitting on. I suddenly wish it was me making her laugh like that.

I notice the bartender nod in my direction. His movement directs Jen's attention my way, and instantly her mesmerizing smile fades. Great. Now I look like some creeper piece of shit. I nod in hello to her and make my way to the bar, taking the seat next to her.

"I didn't realize you would be here," I tell her as I signal to the bartender to bring me the same as what Jen's drinking, a Corona with a lime.

Jen looks away from me, refusing to make sociable eye contact. "I'm not sure why I'm here, actually," she replies before taking a swig of her beer. "I sent the photos to Campbell over a week ago. There really is no reason she should need me here, and she wouldn't tell me over the phone what she wanted. That never bodes well when it comes to Cam."

I'm surprised she's willing to talk to me, even if she refuses to look at me. I take it as a good sign that her hostility toward me has tapered slightly. I want nothing more than to keep her talking so she'll reveal those golden, honey eyes of hers. If I'm asking for things, I think I would prefer this was a two person meeting and the rest of the band would be no-shows. I can't even explain why I'm drawn to the girl; she has been nothing but a thorn in my little toe from the moment I met her. For some reason though, I find myself intrigued by her.

"Helllllloooo? Seriously, Casen, do you have some attention disorder I should be made aware of in regard to speaking with you, or are you just that weird?" she asks.

Well, that's fucking great. She's caught me ogling over her again, and now I look like the team captain of the varsity douche patrol. On a positive note, at least I finally get to see those honey eyes.

"Um, sorry," I tell her, shaking my head and focusing down on my beer. "I was just thinking I would go wherever Campbell told me, whenever she told me to do it. That girl has done more for this band in just a few months, than we've managed to do on our own in two years. I owe her a lot."

"Yeah, well, Cam tends to hide things up her sleeve and then put you in a position to try and make you a better person. Usually her plans fuck up your whole day. I suspect nothing less from this little encounter she has planned for us today."

"What's so bad about being a good person?"

She swivels in her chair and squares her shoulders toward me, taking one final guzzle of her beer before sliding it to the bartender at the end of the bar. "Nothing is wrong with being a good person, if you already are one. It's exhausting to pretend to be something you're not, though. So, I prefer to remain the shell of a person I am, no matter how much Cam wants to change me."

I'm not sure how to respond. I begin to gawk at her again, searching for the right words. Before I can get out any insightful response, I hear her laugh. She pats me on the arm like the dumbshit I'm acting like.

"Now you can forget about wanting me and move on to some band groupie who would be more than happy to fawn over your morally sound ass." With that, she jumps off her chair and walks past me, waving to Campbell and the guys who have finally arrived.

I'm left in stunned silence. Instead of jumping up and joining the group right away, I hang back and watch them find a table and sit down. I need a minute to gather my bearings after our brief exchange. I can't make heads or tails of what she told me, and I can't decide how I feel about it. A part of me certainly wants to run and get as far away from her as possible. She will chew me up and spit me out, she knows it and I know it. Yet a bigger part of me wants to pursue her, find out more about this extremely complex woman. A woman who actually thinks there is nothing of heart and beauty inside of her. I want to prove to her how she's wrong about herself. I want to make her see what Campbell sees, a beautiful person who is rough around the edges and tries to protect whatever has been damaged.

I feel their eyes on me, and sure enough, my bandmates, Jen, and Campbell are all watching me from across the restaurant area of the brewery. Everyone has taken a seat at a booth toward the back of the pub. Yet here I sit like a loser once again, daydreaming about a fucking girl who has done nothing except treat me like shit. Nonetheless, I can't scratch the thought of her out of my head.

As soon as I notice them, I see Jen's head dip behind a menu to shield herself from me. Campbell looks at me with a little concern and I try to deliver my best, 'Dude, I'm cool' look. That is until I see Royce mouth, "What the fuck?" It's the nudge I need to peel my ass off the barstool and head to the meeting. I admit I'm acting completely out of character; they must all think I'm doped up on something herbal, or maybe I'm showing signs of a stroke. Fucking awesome. I need to get my shit together in the fifty paces it will take to get to the table.

"Fuck, dude, if you're high, the polite thing to do is share with the group," Royce chuckles when I finally arrive at the table.

"You're an asshole," I shoot back as he stands to let me into the booth. I slide in while they all take turns making some kind of joke and laugh about my odd behavior. Even Jen laughs, her menu bouncing with each giggle.

"Ha, ha, you guys are so damn hilarious. It's been a long day, that's all. I'm a little zoned out today."

"Okay, boys, playtime's over. I actually brought you here for a reason," Campbell interjects, crossing her arms on the table and mustering her best business expression. This must be a much more serious business conversation than we all thought.

Everyone sits up a little straighter and zeroes in on Campbell and her announcement…except Jen, who remains glued to her menu. My eyes slowly wander from Jen back to Campbell and back again, in an attempt to gauge both of them.

"After the photo shoot, I had flyers and demos made up to send out to media outlets. I plan on sending record labels the same promotional materials to garner more attention for you guys on this mini-tour coming up," she begins. Of course, we all nod, as we knew that was the purpose of the shoot.

Campbell's serious demeanor begins to crack and a devious smile slowly shines through. "Well, let's just say, you have been well received," she says before shifting back into serious Campbell mode.

"Jesus, Cam. Just spit it out already," John sighs, his patience wearing.

"Sorry," she says with a giggle. "Not only has Sony Records inquired about signing you guys for a record deal after the tour, but they want to have a media exposé featuring the band done as a way to roll out the publicity if you sign with them and begin recording under the label." She holds her glass up in the air. "Congratulations, boys. You made it!" she squeals.

There is silence for a moment, as we let her words sink in. We sit with our mouths hanging wide open in complete shock. This announcement is the last thing I think any of us were expecting. For me, there are only two things I've ever wanted, a record deal and a family. Now that I may have one of those, my heart and mind can barely keep up with the emotions I'm feeling.

"Fuck yeah!" Royce excitedly shouts, breaking the silence and allowing all of us permission to celebrate. We stand, hugging and high fiving each other. There are several moments of celebration, before Jen clears her throat and draws our attention back to the table.

"Congratulations and everything. But, um, why in the hell am I here?" she asks Campbell.

Campbell's excitement fades and her serious tone takes effect once more. Cool and collected Cam looks nervous. "You see…the thing is…the label really liked the photos you took." She cringes before continuing with the explanation. Jen begins to catch the drift of what her proposed role is and her brows pull together. "They liked them so much they want the same photographer who took them to follow the band's shows and take all of the pictures for the exposé."

Jen vigorously shakes her head. "Not happening. I'm not some band aide from *Almost Famous*. I'm a professional photographer who did you a favor; believe me, my generosity has been stretched to the max in regards to this band." Her eyes slide to mine as she enunciates the last bit of her sentence. I take the hint. It's not that she's done with the band, she's doesn't want to have to deal with me.

Fuck that. I can't let this opportunity slip through our fingers just because neither of us knows how to handle our attraction for each other. While I turn into a bumbling idiot who is one glue lick away from being required to use safety scissors and wear a teddy bear harness backpack, she wants to scare me away as a way to avoid it altogether. I refuse to let her intimidate me. I plan to chisel away at her frozen exterior, one ice chip at a time.

"Jen, can I speak to you alone for a minute?" I ask her. Somehow, I have to convince her we both can be professional and put whatever it is between us on the back burner or extinguish it entirely. She looks at me like I've grown two heads. She rolls her whisky brown eyes before sliding out of the booth to stand next to me. The guys move out of our way and she ushers me to lead her away from everyone.

The place is beginning to fill up, so finding a quiet space to talk is nearly impossible. I lead her toward the parking lot, where I at least know we won't be interrupted. I look back at the guys to signal to them I'll get everything smoothed out. Royce once again proves himself the king of the dickheads as he dry humps the air. John notices and pushes him back into the booth.

"Oh yeah, how tempting. I can't wait to join the ranks," she sneers after witnessing the immature Royce-ism. Yes, we've actually named the stupid shit he does;

Royce-ism is all we could come up with to cover all of his moments which embarrass the hell out of us.

I don't answer her. Instead, I lightly place my hand on the small of her back and push her toward the exit. The thin, soft fabric of her cotton dress snags on my callused hand, but I refuse to move away from her. I want to savor this small, physical moment, as it might be the only one I ever get.

When we hit cool air and the open space of the outside, she moves away from me to gain some distance. She veers in the direction of her car, but I grab her hand and pull her toward my truck. She looks at me somewhat conflicted, but continues to follow me.

My truck is parked in the back half of the lot; it's my baby and I don't trust the parking skills of the rest of society to not scratch it. I always take extra precautions when it comes to Nelly. Nelly is a black 1956 Ford truck I found at a junkyard, rusted out and missing most of her parts. It took several years and a lot of money, but she is now completely restored.

"Holy shit!" she gasps. "How does a starving musician afford a truck like this?" she asks when we arrive at Nelly.

"I get that a lot," I smirk. "I said I was a musician, but I never said I was starving," I tell her as she walks around the truck, admiring each polished and waxed piece until she meets me at the driver's side door.

"Oh, I get it. You're a spoiled rich kid who has chosen to follow his artistic talents instead of the family business," she huffs. The comment couldn't be further from the truth, and it rubs me the wrong way considering her own upbringing.

I lean up against the side of the truck, careful not to scratch the pristine paint job. "Actually no," I explain. "I was raised by my grandmother on food stamps in a single-wide trailer. I invested what little money I was making once I left home and I did well for myself. I play guitar because I love it. Don't take this the wrong way, but isn't that kind of the pot calling the kettle?"

Her back stiffens and I raise my hands up in surrender. "I don't mean to piss you off, Jen. It just seems pretty shitty to knock me for possibly having money growing up, when I know you did."

"Yes, I had money, Casen," she admits, placing her hands on her hips. "However, while you earned your fortune probably with the support of your family, when I graduated college I walked away from mine. What I have, I earned on my own."

"You know, we really aren't too different from one another. If you weren't so busy protecting the saddle on that high horse of yours, you would see that."

"High horse? High horse? I've only been reacting to your self-absorbed, arrogant comments which you've continuously whirled at me since we met. If anyone has been sabotaging any kind of working relationship, it's you," she spits back.

If I think about our few encounters, half of the time it was me who egged her on and acted in a manner, which resembled pulling a girl's pigtails on the playground.

"I think we are both at fault, yet I also think there is no reason you can't take the job. We're grown-ups, and it's not like you are going to follow us around like some stalker fan. You'll show up to gigs, take some pictures, and go home...just like any other photo shoot."

She begins to mull over her options and, no doubt, her thoughts about me. She then starts moving closer to me, jabbing her finger toward me with each step. "I'm not hanging out with your groupies; I will not photograph any of them. And if you guys, i.e. Royce, can't keep it decent around me I swear on your shriveled dick I'll quit."

Her tirade leaves her only centimeters from me, and I feel her toned body rub against mine with every breath she takes. Her coconut lotion smells so good, I want nothing more than to live in her scent. Towering over her tiny frame, I struggle with my desire to pick her up and spread her out across the hood of Nelly. As much as I want to, I realize it will only complicate our working relationship. Until the tour is over, it's essential to remain friendly yet contained. Before I commit to my new hands-off policy, I need to send her a similar message. When I see her eyes bounce from my eyes to my lips, I know I have the green light to send my message.

I quickly pull her hips toward me and spin her up against the driver's side door. She is taken completely by surprise, but I crash my lips onto hers before she can say or do anything to stop me. Her lips are soft and when I demand more from her she obliges. I grip onto the back of her dress, bunching the fabric in my strong grasp to hold her in place, putting everything I have into this kiss, hoping it will be the first of more to come after the tour.

When I feel her begin to lose to control and melt into me, I quickly pull away. "I don't know why you would think I wouldn't want more of that, but for now you can pretend you don't want me either," I whisper in her ear. I lightly kiss her neck just behind her ear, spin her around, and climb into my truck. I reverse, leaving her there dumbfounded, standing wobbly-legged in the parking lot. I can't help but grin at achieving the task of flustering Jen to the point of both confusion and excitement. I only hope her anticipation wins out in the end.

CASEN

"I think I'm going to throw up," Seiger announces as he rushes through the dressing room to get to the staging area.

John is oblivious with his headphones on. He's been drumming on every hard surface he can find for the past hour. He needs to get ahold of his nerves before we're forced to use a back-up drummer. He won't be able to perform with us because he'll be too busy dislodging the drumstick I'm going to shove up his ass.

Royce strolls into the room while passing Seiger in the doorway, offering a look of confusion. "I don't know what his problem is," he says to me once he's in the dressing room and seated on the table with what little food and drinks have been offered by the venue. It's usually not much, just a package of bottled water, a few pieces of fruit, and a box of whatever cookies were on sale at the local grocery store bakery. Tonight is no different, but to Royce, this is a feast. Whatever is leftover at the end of the night will be packed in his backpack and taken home to fill his cupboards until the next gig...yeah he's that guy. You should see him at hotels. It's embarrassing, the man takes everything but the remote and towels.

"Whether we play well or not, by the way, we always play well, I'm still going to be banging the best lookin' piece of ass here," Royce says between bites of apple. "I don't see why the guys are so uptight tonight; they know I always share the ladies."

I roll my eyes. "How considerate of you, but I don't think they're worried about pulling in the chicks tonight. They want to do well for the tour." My clipped tone reflects my own growing nerves. Tonight's show really is no different than any other we've done over the last two years, but it doesn't make me any less nervous. I know we'll probably perform well and the crowd will love our sound. What has me on edge is the presence of someone in particular this evening. Tonight is Jen's first night with us on tour, and I'm all twisted up over it.

"You on edge too, man?" Royce asks. "It wouldn't be because of a certain little spitfire who will be joining us tonight, is it?"

"She's a pain in my ass. The only thing I care about in regards to her is she stays out of my way so I can do my job and she does the job she's being paid to do," I lie. He has absolutely pegged what I'm all worked up about. A tiny blonde with a sassy mouth and witty comebacks which keep me on my toes is who has me in knots. I would never admit it to him, though.

"Glad to hear that, Thompson. I think with a little extra effort and charm, I can get her to use her camera with me in a not so professional way, if you get my meaning."

I know for a fact Jen would rather live a life of celibacy before she would ever consider sleeping with Royce. If they were the last two people on Earth, she would allow the human race to go extinct. Nonetheless, a spark of jealousy rises up at the thought of the two of them together. My possessiveness for someone who I'm not even with is why I'm not going to give him the heads up about her disdain for him. It will be much more fun watching the humiliating rejection headed his way.

"I don't think it's a good idea for any of us to get involved with her. It needs to stay a working relationship, at least until the tour is over," I lecture, knowing full well he's not going to follow any bit of the advice I offer.

"Yum, wouldn't mind a taste of that kind of work," he responds, using air quotes for the word work.

"You're such a douche," I say, picking up an orange off the table and chucking it at him. "How you have even found one woman to sleep with you is beyond me."

He snags the orange, but briefly fumbles it in his hands before maintaining control of the fruit and tucking it into his side and jumping off the table to model the Heisman stance. "It really is a gift," he says with a crooked smile, pointing to his member. "Women struggle to resist this tuna tornado."

I notice Jen in the doorway taking photos of the spectacle, which is Royce. I find humor in the whole situation, but Jen looks offended. Royce has yet to realize he's being photographed, and has now moved onto humping and spanking the air as though he's king ding-o-ling.

"Well, hello there, Royce," Jen coos. Royce's eyes bolt open and he stills his gyrating. Jen waltzes in, the natural sway of her slender hips causing her baby blue flowing dress to move back and forth, hitting several inches above her knees. It's not the dress I notice though; it's the jeweled cowgirl boots which click against the wooden floor. I know she's the farthest thing from country and her boots are merely for fashion, but good God, do they look sexy on her. So much for me being able to possibly play it cool with her tonight.

She walks past Royce and throws him a present. "I figured you might be in need of some kind of reproductive assistance while I'm with you guys."

He rips open the gift and immediately his brows pull together as he holds up the gift for me to see. "Lady Sally Inflatable Love Doll," I blurt out, reading the packaging.

"Yup, the triple hole version," she adds. "Whenever you feel the need to hit on me, I will kindly direct your attention to old faithful Sally, because these lady parts," she says while circling her vagina, "want nothing to do with your tornado."

I burst out laughing which only pisses Royce off more. He throws his leftover apple core at me and begins to walk out of the dressing room. He stops at the door and returns to the table, picking up the inflatable Sally. "Thank you for the gift, Jen. I needed a new floaty for the hotel swimming pool," he quips and walks out the door toward the stage.

"Do you have any idea what you've done? He really will use that at the Holiday Inn. He's probably already making plans to make me take him to the store to get a swimsuit so he can bring her along to Water World." I shake my head, picturing the bikini he'll pick out and the stares we'll get when he reserves a lawn chair for her. I'm going to have to start my sabotage immediately.

"He needs to know where I stand with him. Sorry if Sally interrupts the groupie prowl." She snaps a quick picture of me pissed about the groupie comment and takes off out of the room. "See ya out there, rock star. Good luck tonight."

Yes, the groupie assumption struck me the wrong way. People always assume since we're in a band, all of us are willing to fuck anyone who shows an interest in the band. That stereotype might fit the notorious Royce, but I resent the assumption. I don't sleep around, I don't use my music to pick up women, and it's disappointing Jen would think so little of me that she would lump me in with Royce.

I do my best to clear my head before grabbing my guitar and make my way to find the others so we can make our group entrance onto the stage. I need to get out there, feel normal again, and use the music to regroup my emotions. Jen has, once again, made a cluster fuck of my psyche.

Sweat is dripping off of me as I walk off stage. The heat of the house lights was almost unbearable during the show, but the crowd was so energizing, I could have stood on the scorching stage all night. Thankfully, Jen was stealthy during the concert, which enabled me to focus on my playing and not her. Now that we're finished for the night, the up-close and personal shots have resumed. I quickly find the nearest, cleanest towel to dry the sweat off and head toward the dressing room to load my guitar in its case. The rest of the guys lag behind, but Jen hurries to catch up to me.

"So what do you guys do now?" she asks, taking a picture of me wiping my face of the leftover beads of sweat.

"I'm sure you have your own ideas of how the rest of our night plays out; you want to tag along?" I challenge. Other than Royce, our evenings are extremely tame unless Jen considers a few beers, videos games, movie marathons, and camping trips out of hand. Provoking her is a little more fun than telling her the truth, at least for a while.

I open the door to the dressing room, now sans-food, and leaning against the back wall is the perfect person to assist me in my Jen provocation. Stacy has been an uninvited fixture with the band for the past few months. She's a sweet girl, it's just too bad she doesn't value herself more than a musician's evening companion. She's offered the goods repeatedly to everyone, but Royce is the only one who has cashed in the offer—repeatedly.

"Casen, there you are!" she exclaims, her voice reminiscent of one of those chicks from Clueless. My IQ plummets each time she speaks to me. She's jumping up and down and her tits flail about like they are fighting each other to escape the garment prison she's trapped them in. I use the term garment loosely. Her double Ds aren't held in place by a bra, although her tiny shirt looks similar to one. She's paired it with cutoff jean shorts. The pockets hang down out the front, which suggests if she turns around, we'll be greeted by Stacy's butt folds. She runs to me, hopping into my arms and landing a kiss on my cheek. I turn with her in my arms to face Jen and, judging from her expression, I was dead-on with my butt cheek assessment. She's caught so off guard, it takes her a moment to remember her camera.

"Hello, Stacy," I respond unenthusiastically. "Did you enjoy the show?" I drop her to the ground as Jen clears her throat.

"Are you going to introduce me to your little friend?" Jen inquires. I can tell she thinks she's nailed it, that I'm a groupie hound and Stacy's presence proves it. I sense a bit of jealousy as well, though. This is the perfect situation to sour her mood.

"Sorry. This is—"

"Stacy," she interrupts, stepping in front of me to shake Jen's hand. "I hang out with the band sometimes." Then she rounds on me. "By the way, Mr. Guitar Man, you know I don't mind sharing, but the least you could do is ask."

Jen's expression is priceless, she could catch flies with the way her mouth hangs open. To her credit, she recovers quickly. "I'm not here to sleep with anyone," she says, holding up her camera.

"Fuck, Casen, you know I have rules about photography," Stacy huffs, placing hands on her curvy hips. "You always ask a girl first, but I guess for you I can make an exception." She begins to stride toward me, a smile lighting up her face. Before I can correct any part of the situation, Jen takes the room's climate from slight breeze to hurricane status.

"So your primary role here is to service the band, roadies, bartenders, and anyone in need of a vagina?" Jen snips as she clicks away on her camera. "Is this a new business/social venture or have you always been into trying to land wealthy men with your physical assets?"

Stacy may not be the brightest, but she understands immediately that Jen is calling her out. The claws come out and I'll begin to fear for my life if I don't intervene or get Royce in here to help separate the ladies into their opposing corners.

"Are you kidding me? Who the hell do you think you are?" Stacy asks. I'm waiting for fire to begin shooting out of her mouth, like one of the dragons from Harry Potter.

"Make no mistake, I didn't mean to offend." Click goes Jen's camera. "I'm actually intrigued." Click, click.

"Would you please put that camera down before I shove it up your ass?"

Oh, damn, I'm about to be responsible for a chick fight. I need to de-escalate! "Royce!" I shout into the hallway. "There is someone here to see you."

Hearing he has possible company for the evening, even if it's just Stacy, he rushes into the room. He abruptly stops when he sees the estrogen-overdosed scene before him.

"Actually, I'm doing a photo shoot for the CDC in the next few weeks for their new VD posters. I think you would be a perfect model for it," Jen says as politely and sweetly as possible. The true meaning of what she's implying flies entirely over Stacy's head and her demeanor changes immediately.

"Really, a model? You think so?" she asks, her tone full of hope, her eyes brightening up with the possibility of a modeling career. Royce doubles over with laughter and I know as soon as he catches his breath, he will crush her hopes.

"All right, Jen, it's time to go, we have that reservation to get to." I grab her by the arm and pull her out of the room before she can resist.

"Casen has my number," Stacy shouts after us as we exit. "Call me!"

I quickly close the door, averting the crisis.

"Is that the dramatics you were after?" Jen asks as we walk down the hallway toward the parking lot.

"Not exactly." I pin her with my eyes. "Come on, it's still early, I'm taking you out."

"I'm good, thanks," she shoots back, pulling out of my grip.

"Get over yourself, sparkplug. It's not a date; we're going to go blow off some steam." I hold open the backdoor to the venue for Jen and the warm spring air slams into us. There was a storm the evening before, so the humidity is high. A perfect night for what I have in mind for us.

Jen

"You have got to be shittin' me," I say as we pull into the gravel parking lot. "You realize we aren't thirteen, right? We're adults."

Casen puts the pickup in park; a truck I think he has the strangest, almost unhealthy, relationship with, and he looks to me with a shit-eating grin. "Just because we're almost thirty, doesn't mean we need to act like it all the time. I know you're not the boring type, sparky. Get out of the truck, we're having some fun tonight."

I'm always a girl up for a good time, but I haven't been to a carnival since I was a freshman in high school. The lights of the death traps for rides brighten the night sky as waves of teenagers fill the fairgrounds, racing from one electronic adventure to the next. None of it makes me want to hop out and run to the Tilt-a-Whirl. Standing in a crowded line with a bunch of horny, zit-faced teenagers is not my idea of a rip-roaring good time

Casen runs around the front of the truck and opens my door. What a gentleman, too bad I'd have just as much chance of needing a tetanus shot whether I went near a carnival ride or his man parts. He swings open the passenger door, and the smell of cotton candy, popcorn, and roasted peanuts fill my nostrils, tickling me with temptation.

"Get your ass out of the truck, sparkplug," he says, holding his hand out for me to take. "We're going to have us some fun."

Smacking his hand away, I jump down out of the truck. "No twisty, spinning rides which may end my life and you're buying me as much junk food as I can hold down." I turn to him, looking for agreement.

"You got it, but you owe me one round on the bumper cars," he says, shutting the truck door behind me.

The bumper cars sound like the perfect way to let out some of the pent-up frustration I have for this man. Instead of admitting my friends are right and I like Casen, I find it easier to pretend he brings out my homicidal tendencies. The bumper cars sound ideal; where else can I act out my road rage fantasies and legally rear-end someone?

Walking side by side, we slowly approach the chaos. I giggle at Casen as the jittery excitement I'm containing spills out. The sirens and screams from the rides mix with the buzzers of the games area and the overwhelming noise begins to crowd my senses. My eyes widen at the sight, which includes carnies ready to swindle me out of a dollar, funnel cakes, and ring toss for a gold fish prize. All I need now is a margarita stand and I would squeal.

"I thought you were too old for such childish things?" Casen asks, when he notices my enthusiasm.

I rein in a grin before answering, which probably makes me look even worse. "Well, I figure if I'm going to spend the evening with you and a bunch of hormonal teenagers, I might as well drink the Kool-Aid and enjoy myself. Besides, I could never pass up the opportunity to beat your ass at ring toss."

"Sure, sure," he laughs. "Whoever gets the biggest stuffed animal wins. Loser buys the winner a funnel cake. Sound like a fair wager?"

I let my eyes scan over the rows of games, sizing up my best options. "Biggest stuffed animal or the most prizes?" I ask for clarification.

"Biggest." He folds his arms across his chest waiting for my answer. I stare at the intricate designs of his tattoos splayed across his tanned, toned arms. They are beautiful to look at and for a split second, I think about what it would feel like to have them wrapped around me.

Unfortunately, I know his mouth would probably ruin my warm, fuzzy moment.

"And you can't buy the prize, it must be won," he adds when he notices my devious grin, albeit for a different reason than he thinks.

"Of course. No cheating. Game's on, sucker," I agree, lightly pushing on his stone hard chest. I wonder if those tattoos merge onto his chiseled chest. *Fuck, Jen, get your lady parts under control,* I tell myself, quickly pulling my hand back and letting it hang at my side.

We both buy a bundle of tickets and rush to the bumper cars. We figure it's better to get the assault and battery out of the way before we begin hauling around the massive amount of prizes we both plan to win. I'm sure we're both overestimating our ability to out-play the carnie-folk who learn from birth how to rig a game so no one ever wins, but nonetheless, we are confident.

Handing the operator my ticket, I rush through the gate and select my vehicle of mayhem. "I want the green one!" I shout, jumping into the driver's seat and buckling the seat belt. It seems like an oxymoron to have safety restraints on a ride in which the purpose is to knock the shit out of the other participants using an electric car the size of a Power wheel. "Prepare for a week of whiplash, Thompson," I tease as he climbs into a blue car with yellow racing stripes. I can't help but smile at this man who seems so carefree. He's not like me. He isn't hiding; he's not afraid to truly be with someone. He hasn't restrained his heart to protect it from the whiplash of love. No, Casen is nothing like me.

The cars are filled with people, but there is only one particular car I zero in on when the operator flips the switch to bring the cars to life. The poles connecting the cars to the ceiling spark and buzz as the cars move around the roller-skating rink arena. I press on the accelerator and turn the wheel in the direction of Casen. Moving behind a group of other riders, I'm hoping for an initial surprise attack; it may be the only good shot I get at him. I swing around the cluster of people, only to realize I've lost him in the crowd. I search the cars looking for the blue car with recognizable yellow stripes and I come up empty.

Then out of nowhere, my body lurches forward, my face nearly hitting the foam steering wheel. I now have an appreciation for the harness I mocked not more than five minutes ago. I rub my neck and look behind me to verbally bash the culprit, only to see Casen there. He took a play from my bumper-car playbook and used it against me...asshole.

"Looks like you may need a refresher course on the purpose of bumper-cars, sparkplug," he says as cocky as ever. "I think you confused it with go-carts."

"Very funny," I snap. "You just watch your ass, speed-racer." I narrow my eyes at him and rocket around him. Turning in a circle, I race toward him and slam into the side of his car, sending him crashing into the side of his vehicle. He frowns at me, almost stunned that I took a shot at him. I pretend to be innocent of any wrongdoing, but I immediately smile on the inside.

We spend the remainder of the five-minute ride evading each other while occasionally bumping into others around us unintentionally. That is, until we notice a teenage boy purposely knocking into all of the younger kids on the ride. He knows none of them and is intentionally broadsiding any kid smaller than him; some have even started to cry. Casen and I look to one another and without speaking, we both know what to do with this little shit. We circle in opposite directions in order to outflank deputy dipshit. Timing it perfectly, we accelerate and slam into either side of the teen's car, bouncing from Casen's then to mine like a ping-pong ball. I wanted to yell, 'Score! Man down,' but I instead I try to act my age. It's difficult, but I do my best.

"Young man, are you okay? That was a hard hit," I ask him, acting as concerned as possible considering my limited acting skills.

He looks pissed at first, rubbing his neck. "Jeeeez, it's like you tried to hit me on purpose."

"Dude, you know you're on the bumper-cars, right? If you were looking for non-contact, there's a go-cart place just down the road," Casen interjects. His eyes slide to mine and I try to hide my smile at the same words he used on me.

"Whatever, you guys suck. Aren't you a little old to be at a carnival without kids?" dingle berry says as he walks away. As soon as he's out of sight, I finally let out the laugh I'd been holding in.

"I told you we were too old to be here," I tell Casen through laughter.

"Why, because the teenage bully we just gave a lesson to said so? Yeah, I'm gonna go with bullshit on that one," he jokes.

Casen places his hand on my back and leads me through the exit of the arena. His hand feels like fire; however, his touch is not a burn I would shy away from. It's a warmth which makes me want to snuggle into him and seek more of. I fight through the feeling and move away from him. I know better than to get into a relationship, especially with a guy like Casen. I'm great at flings, give me a week or maybe two and it's a magical time filled with awesome sex. I don't venture into anything more than that. More would require honesty; it would require sharing the real me with someone. I can't risk the emotional crippling of rejection; so instead, I sacrifice relationships for casual encounters. They are safer, easier. For the last decade safe and easy is all I've wanted.

Casen and I hit game stand after game stand, cashing in our tickets. I say cashing in because that's exactly what it's like. We paid for the tickets just to hand said tickets right back to the person running the game, without ever getting anything in return. My luck sucked, but at least Casen hasn't been much better. He's toting around a tiny stuffed rabbit he won at the baseball throw.

It's not until we walk up on the ball toss when I feel my luck turn around. The objective is to toss a ball into wooden baskets. The catch? The baskets are propped up in a way, which favors finesse and not strength. Most of the time the ball will bounce right out.

It's do or die time. Pulling the hair tie off my wrist, I throw my hair into a messy bun. I need to make this last ticket count. "You want to go first?" I ask, trying not to show my frustration.

"No, you go right on ahead," he says, handing his ticket over to me. "Here's my ticket, too. I think you may need all the help you can get."

I take his ticket and tear it up. "You're an ass, and now neither of us can use it. You better hope Peter Cottontail can hold up a little longer."

Giving the carnie behind the booth counter a thorough once over, I hand the little red stub over to him. His grimy clothes, oily hair, and yellowing teeth fit the name plastered across his faded nametag. Bart, like the pirate. A pirate that wants to steal my last chance at victory. The only prizes available are humungous teddy bears. Why? You get three balls and all three have to make it into the baskets to win. A person is lucky to get one in, thus the lure of the big prize. Bart slides the bucket filled with three whiffle balls to me and instructs me to take my time. Yeah, time is what I need to win; thanks for the tip, Bart.

Picking up the first whiffle ball, my fingers twisting into the holes of the ball, I concentrate on the baskets. Taking aim, I delicately toss the ball toward the center and it settles at the bottom of the basket. "Fuck ya!" I shout when I see the ball isn't going to bounce out. "One down, Mr. Thompson," I brag.

I swipe ball number two from the bucket and repeat my previous technique. I'm met with the same positive results. Only one ball sits between victory and me. I eagerly pick up the final ball and take my aim. Just as I'm about to release it, Casen leans in and whispers, "Don't choke." The jerk even blows in my ear.

"You cheated!" I yell, as the ball bounces out of the basket and rolls across the dirt.

"You weren't concentrating. If you really wanted to win, you would have," he explains, turning and walking in the direction of the food carts.

I'm left stunned with anger beginning to roll off me. Realizing I'm being left behind, I race to catch up to him at the funnel cake stand. "That's a load of shit and you know it."

"Maybe," he laughs. "But I couldn't help it; I couldn't get beat by a girl."

I roll my eyes; I know damn well Casen doesn't care if he loses to a girl. He just wanted to piss on my parade.

Casen takes a look around and finds a little girl nearby and offers her his rabbit. He even asks the girl's parents first. I'm sure if Carly or Vivian were here, their hearts would have melted and their ovaries would have had a heart attack, but not me. My first thought is, *you're not supposed to take gifts from strangers, little girl.* What kind of parents are these to let some random, thirty-something guy give their kid a stuffed animal at a carnival, when said guy doesn't even have kids with him? It screams Dateline special on how to catch a predator.

"Now neither of us has a prize, we're even," he says when he returns from his creepy good deed.

"I guess so. I say we buy our own funnel cakes. You're without a prize, and I'm not nice to cheaters," I tell him before filing into the funnel cake line.

After we each take our turn buying our snacks and find seats on a set of nearby hay bales, we both dig into the confectionary goodness, which is no doubt rotting my teeth with every bite.

"So, Stacy, huh?" I ask, shoving another piece of bread into my mouth, powdered sugar leaving a trail on my chin. "You guys all just take your turn passing her around or what?"

He chokes on his funnel cake and it takes him a moment to catch his breath. "I've never been with Stacy, not for a lack of trying on her part. I told you, I don't sleep around, Jen," he responds and then wipes the sugar off my chin.

"But you hang with Royce and you have to admit that guy has had more 'tang than an astronaut." Casen bursts into laughter at my critique of his friend.

"Royce really isn't that bad of a guy, but I'm nothing like him when it comes to women. You need to understand the difference between him and me. While Royce is looking for a girl for the night, I'm looking for a girl for the rest of my life." I try to let his comparison sink in, but before I can respond, Casen gathers our trash and once again offers his hand to me. "Come on, I'll take you back to your car. Thank you for hanging out with me tonight. I hope this means we've called a truce and can be friends."

I don't say anything. Instead, I smile and slide my hand into his. That's all I need to show him. My hand tucked in his provides a sense of security that I never thought I could tolerate, let alone seek out. Just for a moment, I can feel those restraints unbuckle and my heart beats wildly at the idea of a relationship with Casen, but then my mind gains control again, and snaps those emotions back into place. The risk is too daunting.

JEN

Shit, shit, shit! I pride myself on my ability to be on time to appointments. Correction; I pride myself on the effort I put into trying to be on time to events. I'm usually late, but I try hard not to be. Tonight is no damn different. It's only the third show in the tour and I, once again, have found arranging the "perfect" outfit to tease Casen has proven elusive and is now the cause for my tardiness.

Tonight is a bigger show in Colorado Springs with several bands performing throughout the evening. The venue is large, the crowd is supposed to be large, and the media attention leading up to it has been large. Being late is not good.

I manage to find a parking spot in the crowded lot behind the venue, which is filled with tour buses, roadies, and the inevitable groupies/fans who are loitering in the back section of the lot, waiting for their chance to "see" the bands.

Slamming my little Camry into park and grabbing my camera bag, I rush toward the back entrance for employees-only as quickly as my skirt and heels will allow. It's not until I reach the security gate and the burly guard when I realize I don't have my crew pass which will allow me on the lot behind the scenes. What a perfect cherry on top to my shit-evening-sundae.

"Sorry, I forgot my badge; do you have a list or something for approved personnel?" I ask as I approach the guard. He's somewhat intimidating, more large than muscular, but bigger than me nonetheless. He has a bit of a haggard appearance with shaggy hair and a few days' worth of facial hair growth. As I get closer I smell alcohol on him, which if the guys in the band or Campbell knew about, he would be tossed out on his ass quicker than Royce could charm the panties off one of the girls waiting at his bus.

"Sorry, honey. No badge, no entrance; those are the rules," he replies as his eyes scan my body, probably appraising whether I'm someone of importance or just some well-dressed groupie. "But you know, with a little persuasion, I've been known to bend the rules a little," he adds, moving closer to me and placing a hand on my ass.

I quickly bat his hand away. "Not interested, asshole. Do I look like the type who would fuck some random limp-dick roadie just for entrance into a small-time concert?"

His breath is warm and acidic, breathing heavily on me as he considers his next chess move. I don't back down though, not from this fuckwad who thinks he can push me around. However, he surprises the hell out of me when he grabs my hand and places it on his dick.

"I think you look like a slut who's pretending she wouldn't fuck anyone who would get her want she wants. And, I would say, right now, you want entrance into this concert. I also think you'll find there is nothing limp about this situation."

His other hand once again finds my ass, squeezing and rubbing it so hard that I realize I'm outmatched and I need to back away from the situation. I move my hand away from his less than impressive area, rear my knee back as much as I can in his grasp, and kick him in the junk hard enough to double him over and cause blunt force trauma to his little swimmers.

"I said I wasn't interested, dipshit," I say, taking a step away from him as he catches his breath. I refuse to leave, if anything I'll call one of the guys and have them meet me at the gate to let me in.

When he finally gathers his bearings, he stands and the look on his face sends an uncomfortable chill up my back; rage is radiating off of him. "You bitch," he roars as he raises his hand and slams it across my face, sending me flying to the unforgiving asphalt. An explosion of pain spreads throughout my cheek and the ground rips open the skin on my knee. I feel the blood begin to drip down my leg.

I'm left on the ground, stunned. I've never been struck before and I don't know how to respond. I don't want to exacerbate the situation by verbally attacking him further, but I don't want to run away and let this go as if I accept what he's done as acceptable. I'm only on the ground for a few seconds, with no chance to make up my mind on my course of action, before he's picking me up and pulling me by my hair toward a shadowed part of the gate.

I let out as much of a scream as I can muster, recognizing this might be my only chance to call for help. "Shut the fuck up," he huffs, as he throws me against the fence, pinning me between it and his chest. His fingers are twisted into my hair, holding me in place, my battered face being scraped further by the metal of the fence.

"Please," I plead. "Please stop." I try to wiggle out of his grasp but he's too strong. His acidic, beer breath is hot on my neck and it turns my stomach. I continue to struggle until I feel his free hand moving under my skirt ripping at my panties. My body tenses and panic overwhelms me.

"Women like you need to be taken down a few notches," I hear him whisper "I plan on teaching you a fucking lesson."

My brain begins to shut off to the present, making way for the images of the night that changed everything. It was an event I could never truly remember, but the scenes in the photographs are something I could never forget. They flood my head, taking over.

Before his hands can violate my body further, the weight forcing me against the fence is gone and I slide down until I'm sitting on the ground, huddled against the jagged metal, gripping onto it for safety.

My eyes are pinched shut, but somehow tears have managed to escape and are sliding down my face. I feel completely out of control as my body shakes with adrenaline, but still I refuse to release the safety of the chain-link. When I feel hands on my face and then smoothing through my hair, the sensation causes me to yell out and move closer to the fence, even though there is no possible way to get any closer without climbing it.

"Shhh, sweetheart. You're safe now," a smooth, baritone voice that has become so familiar to me whispers…Casen. I know it's him, but I can't seem to let myself peel away from the fence.

"I'm here, Jen. Let go, baby, I'm here," Casen continues as he tries to pull me away from the gate.

The blood rushes back to my fingers when I release my grip on the slick metal. My thumbs run along the indentations to soothe the throbbing sensation. Casen immediately slides me onto his lap and I burrow myself into his chest.

"What the fuck happened here, man?" I hear Royce shout.

"What the fuck do you think happened, Royce?" he replies as he begins to stand with me in his arms. "Call the police to get this piece of shit out of here. I'm taking her with me." It's only then I finally open my eyes and the sight before me causes a sob to break loose. My attacker is on the ground, unconscious and bleeding. I can't see them, but I'm sure I would find large gashes on Casen's knuckles, judging from the damage his hands caused.

"No, no police," I tell him. His strong stride instantly stops.

"We have to call the police, he needs to go to jail for this," he says soothingly, holding me close.

I respond by shaking my head adamantly. I may not give a shit about my horrible parents, but I'm smart enough to know not to venture under their radar. "If there are police reports, there will be media attention. Please, I just want to leave."

Casen dips his head and sighs after an excruciatingly long pause. I know he's going against his better judgment by respecting my wishes, and if he were calling the shots here there would be about a million police cars circling this back lot.

"Okay," he finally says before turning back around to face Royce. "Don't call the police, Royce, just get this shit bag off the lot and see to it that he won't be working any more venues. Whatever Deputy Dewey badge he has, I want it revoked."

"No fucking way, we need to call the authorities, and what in the hell am I supposed to do with this guy? What about the show, man?" Royce asks.

Casen tightens his grip on me and takes a deep breath before letting out a bellow, which makes me startle in his arms. "Dammit, Royce, just fucking handle this!" he shouts, taking a step closer to him. "Tell Campbell I had some kind of emergency and she'll find a stand-in for the night. Either way, I'm leaving and taking Jen with me."

Without giving Royce the opportunity to argue, he storms off in the direction of his truck. I don't protest, I don't request he take me to my car. I go willingly with him, handing over every bit of control I usually demand from a situation. Casen makes me feel safe and taken care of, a feeling I rarely have felt in my life. My parents couldn't protect me, my friends have never known I needed protection, yet Casen has somehow stepped in and given me what I needed in the exact moment I needed it.

Once in the passenger seat and on the road, the lights of the city begin to fade. As the dark landscape of the mountains envelops us, I allow my mind to finally process the events of the evening. Thankfully, Casen doesn't bombard me with questions or pepper me with insistent probing into my well-being. He stays quiet, merely holding my hand to show his support; it's like he knows that is all I need or even want right now.

The darkness and lack of conversation forces my mind to be overtaken by the resurfaced memories of my tainted past and the terrifying events which occurred this evening. I'm conflicted by feelings of appreciation as well as embarrassment that Casen was there to see and save me in such a vulnerable moment. As much as I don't want Casen to see me struggle, I can't keep my tears at bay. They slowly run down my cheeks and when Casen hears my sniffles, he squeezes my hand, but continues to remain silent. I'm so emotionally exhausted it soon becomes a challenge to keep my eyes open. It isn't long before I feel the calmness of sleep pull me under.

CASEN

As soon as we get to the camper I keep parked at Mueller State Park, I carry a sleeping Jen to the back bedroom and make a bed for myself on the foldout couch. As much as I want to sleep, I'm unsuccessful, tossing and turning until I force myself out of bed to get things ready for Jen in the morning.

I don't know how I contained myself from killing that guy. Lord knows I fucking wanted to. Since that was off the table, I at least wanted him arrested. I was more than shocked when Jen wouldn't let me call the authorities. I really don't know what to do for her; I don't know how to fix any of this, fix her—but I want to. It's apparent she's been through some kind of shit in her life...haven't we all? This is different though, she's hiding something. I've always been able to tell when someone was running, when they've buried secrets, and Jen MacLauchlan has buried something vicious.

All night I've wandered into the bedroom to watch her sleep, to smooth her hair when her sleep talking and rambles turn into frightened night terrors. My Great Dane, Hendrix, hasn't left her side, alerting me of her terrors with whimpering. I think they upset him as much as they upset me to witness.

When I can't handle the restlessness and useless feelings I have any longer, I lay out a pair of sweats and a T-shirt on the bed for when she wakes up. I write her a note and leave her in the care of Hendrix. I hop into Nelly and head toward Woodland Park. It's the nearest town to the campsite with a Walmart where I can at least pick her up a few toiletry items, some clothes, and medical supplies to clean up my knuckles and her scraped-up knees. Also, I have some food in the camper, but definitely not enough to serve her a proper breakfast and sustain us both for the entire weekend. She may not intend to stay with me longer than the hour to travel back to Colorado Springs where her car is parked, but if I have my way, she will stay the weekend.

It's still early by the time I return, and she's still asleep. I don't want to wake her by continuing my restless hovering, so I busy myself outside by bandaging my knuckles. I then set to work making a campfire and preparing bacon and eggs to make over the open flame. It isn't long after getting everything on the griddle when a bloodcurdling scream from the inside of the camper pierces the morning silence.

I move as quickly as I can, bursting through the front door and down the small hallway to the bedroom. The screams continue, and I prepare for the worst as I turn the door handle to enter the bedroom. The scene before me is not what I expect and I barely contain my laughter.

"Get it off me!" Jen shouts. "I'm covered in slobber!" she continues as she struggles to find her way out of the blankets. Somehow, Hendrix has made his way under the covers with her, to snuggle no doubt...he never got the memo he's too big to be a lap dog. Together they are rolling around, tangled in sheets, Jen frantically trying to get away, and Hendrix trying to lick her. When Jen finally falls out of the bed onto the floor and out of the grips of the flannel sheets, Hendrix halts his slobber attack and barks at her.

"Henri, enough, boy. Outside," I warn. He immediately jumps off the bed and trots past me to go outside by the fire. "Sorry, about that. He's a snuggler; he was trying to tell you he likes you," I explain.

"Likes me? Are you stoned? That giant horse dog was trying to attack me. My hair is matted with dog drool. If I had exposed my neck, he probably would have punctured my jugular." She's being a tad overdramatic. I absolutely want to continue to laugh at her, but considering the events of the previous evening, I would prefer to not upset her.

"He really is harmless. I left clothes on the bed for you. Go ahead and get dressed and come outside, I have breakfast cooking for us," I say before leaving the room, closing the door behind me. Her morning wake-up call was a little unorthodox, and more than likely a little inappropriate considering the circumstances, but at least it broke up any awkwardness I thought there might be between us this morning.

I'm taking everything off the fire and pouring her a cup of coffee when she finally emerges from the camper. My clothes completely swallow her; she has to hold up the sweats with one of her hands to prevent them from falling off. I've never seen Jen so tattered. She's a person who prides herself on her appearance, and right now she is a matted mess. Besides the ridiculously large clothes, her makeup is smeared across her face from crying and sleeping, a bruised cheek matches the smudged makeup, and her hair looks similar to a nest we may find on a hike later today. She would find her appearance unacceptable, but to be honest, I rather like it. It makes her human…imperfectly perfect.

Hendrix immediately perks up when he hears her, but she shoots him a crusty look. "I'm not speaking to you, Goliath," she hisses. Henri whines and settles back down next to my chair.

"I'm glad you've been introduced to Hendrix, he goes by Henri for short." That earns me the crusty look she had reserved for Henri. "Here, I made you a cup," I say, handing her a mug filled with enough caffeine to kill a small horse. "Take a seat and I'll make you some breakfast."

She accepts the mug with her empty hand and slides into the nearest chair. "Thank you," she says meekly with her eyes downcast, refusing to meet mine. The awkwardness I was worried about has invaded our campsite. She closes her eyes and takes a deep inhale of the coffee, letting the warmth of the steam filter around her cheeks. Bringing her knees up under her in the chair, she settles in and begins to stare into the hypnotizing flames of the campfire. I know her mind is everywhere except here, so I hastily fix her plate to provide a distraction from the thoughts overshadowing her.

"Eat up," I tell her as I hand her a plate filled with fried eggs and bacon. "You're going to need energy for what we are doing today," I add, taking a seat in the chair across the fire from her.

She gives me a confused, suspicious look and then laughs, sitting up straight in her chair. "Look, I appreciate what you did for me and giving me the night to regroup, but I'm not going to spend the day doing some counseling session with you filled with outdoorsy activities. If I need a little cardio, I have a gym for that. If I need a group pity party, I have friends for that. All I need right now from you is a ride back to the Springs to get my car so I can drive home."

I pretend to ignore her, taking a large bite of food, and throwing a piece of bacon to Henri. "No can do, Jen," I tell her, focusing my attention on my dog and not her. "I have some things I need to do up here this weekend which you could help with. Besides, your phone has been blowing up since we left last night. I wouldn't think you would be in any hurry to get back to be hit with a million questions." I finally look at her as I shove another mouthful in and talk around the massive amount of food. "I figure, by you staying, you're helping us both out."

Jen sits quietly, contemplating my proposition and what is waiting for her back home. "Fine," she relents. "But I need to call the girls and let them know where I am and that I'm okay. Fuck, I would never hear the end of it, or worse, they'll show up here."

"I took care of it," I say, throwing another piece of bacon to Henri.

"What do you mean, you took care of it?" she asks. "Jesus, quit feeding that dog bacon, he's already the size of a fucking elephant. I thought you weren't supposed to feed animals human food anyways."

"I called Campbell this morning while you were sleeping and filled her in on how you were okay and with me. Told her we would be back Sunday and everyone needed to give you a little space until then. And no, you aren't supposed to feed animals human food. But Hendrix isn't like other dogs; he's a part-human part-elephant, gorilla dog with super strength. He can have something special every now and then."

"Yeah, well, you're going to give him a heart attack," she adds, taking another bite of her food. "So, Campbell was okay with your little plan?"

"She seemed to be. The other women in the background, not so much. There was a lot of shouting and demands to see you, but Campbell smoothed it out."

"Yeah, that doesn't surprise me about Vivian and Carly. They were probably already packed and in the car. I'll be sure to call or text them."

"I wouldn't be surprised if they're camped out at your apartment when you get back to Denver on Sunday night," I laugh. I can only imagine what Campbell had to do or say to calm those women down, but I knew it was a bag full of drama Jen didn't need right now. The air needed to settle before the mother hens were allowed to hover.

"Well, they care about me, even if it can be a little smothering. We're each other's family. I wouldn't trade them for the world. Besides, did I hear you say Sunday night? What in the hell do you need help with that we can't take care of this morning and be back by tonight?" Jen places her mug and plate on the ground and settles in for an argument. I stuff the remainder of my breakfast in my mouth and stand to gather the dishes, ignoring her confrontational posture. "I have things I need to get back to, and I have no clothes. I can't exactly wear your nasty sweats for the next day and a half," she huffs.

She watches as I pick up her dishes and move toward the camper. "It's taken care of, Jen. I went to Walmart this morning and picked you up some things," I say over my shoulder and then whistle for Henri to follow me.

"What?" she shouts.

I hear her stumbling out of her chair in an attempt to chase after me, and Henri immediately begins to bark at her. I struggle to maintain a straight face, picturing the scene unfolding behind my back. When I look back, she's picking herself off the ground and attempting to hold onto the sweats which are falling off her while at the same time ward off Henri who is trying to lick her.

"Do I look like the type of girl who has ever stepped foot in a Walmart? Do they even have clothes?" she asks, as she bats Henri away and finds her footing to stand up.

"Hendrix, come here," I command. He whimpers, but reluctantly leaves her side and goes inside the camper. "No, princess, you certainly don't look like someone who would ever step foot in a Walmart. Maybe you should spend a little more time learning how the other half lives so the fall off your high horse wouldn't hurt so badly."

I immediately turn and enter the camper, closing the door behind me. I know I'm provoking her a tad, but I figure feisty Jen needs to return. If I take the white gloves off and treat her like I always do, maybe her fire will ignite once again. My guess is spot on when I hear the camper door slam as I'm placing the dishes in the sink.

"What in the hell is that supposed to mean?" she shouts. "I'm a completely down to Earth person. Dammit, I go through my closet every year and send things to Goodwill for fuck's sake. Just because I don't like to prance my ass around Wally World so I can have my picture taken and put on those stupid people of Walmart Facebook collages which everyone laughs at doesn't make me a snob. Excuse me for not wanting to be featured on Tosh.0."

With that, I burst into laughter. Hendrix is caught off guard and begins to howl. I'm glad Jen's found her spunk, even if it's to tell me off. Damn that was funny.

"What? What's so funny?" she asks in an agitated tone. "It's pretty rude to laugh at people, you know."

"Oh, sparky, believe me there is nothing funny about this. I try to help you by bringing you here. I try to be considerate by getting you things I think you'll need during your stay at the only place available to me, and you find it's not good enough. I find that rude."

"Ugh! You're infuriating," she announces after letting my words sink in a bit. "I do appreciate what you're doing and I know I can act like a brat at times. I'm sorry, I'm a little out of my element here. I've never done a lot of things, including camping."

"Now that is funny. You've never been camping?" I laugh, but I almost find her confession somewhat sad. What person has never camped out under the stars? There were times as a kid I had no choice but to sleep outside to get away from what was happening at home. The drugs, the fights, the strangers coming in and out of the house; the outdoors was the only safe haven for my siblings and me. Sometimes, getting them to our secret campsite was the only way to keep them safe.

"Spoiled rich kid, remember?" she jests as she plops down onto the seat next to the small kitchen table and uses her finger to circle her face. "Really, though, my father never had time for things like that, and my mother wouldn't be caught dead sleeping in a tent."

"Well then why don't you simmer a little and take this weekend as a time to not only regroup but have a new experience?"

She takes a moment to consider my offer, and I know she'll cave. For all of the tough attitude Jen presents to the world, I know underneath all of the gruffness, is something fragile, something soft which needs nurturing. More and more I find myself wanting to be the man who protects that glass heart of hers...the one who glues her pieces back together.

"Okay, truce," she says, holding her hand out to me. Leaning against the counter I try to act nonchalant about the fact she is willingly staying with me and will be a good sport about all of the outdoor activities she'll be involved in today, but really I'm shaking with excitement. I want to make today unforgettable, help to erase the events of last night. When she closes her eyes tonight, I want her to see me and only me, not that piece of shit security guard.

I push off the counter and reach for her hand to accept the armistice. When she places her hand in mine, instead of shaking it, I pull her from the chair and to my body.

"I promise we will have a good weekend together, Jen," I say, placing my hand on her back and pulling her even closer. "I plan to erase every memory of the nightmare of last night," I whisper in her ear. Her breathing catches as my breath hits her neck, and I know I have her. I move away and slap her ass playfully. "So, get dressed in your damn Walmart camping clothes and get ready for an adventure!"

She squeals and lets out a huff, but then does what I ask, moving past me to the back bedroom. Just before reaching the door, she turns around to face me with a smile to match my own. "You're an asshole, Casen Thompson, don't forget that, but I do appreciate this."

"I do my best, sparkplug," I tell her with a nod before she turns and enters the bedroom, closing the door behind her.

JEN

By the time I make it out of the camper, the dishes have all been cleaned up and Casen is sitting on the back of his truck with the dog. I don't remember his name; Goliath fits him just fine for me. I managed to put myself together, with what I'm assuming are the best pieces in the Mary-Kate and Ashley collection. I'm impressed he remembered the small items like deodorant and a toothbrush. The average male would have forgotten such things and then insisted I use my finger with a little toothpaste and his Axe Body Spray to freshen up.

I want to hate Casen. I want to not want him, but when he does things for me which no other man has ever even thought to do, it makes it damn difficult. I might actually choke on the words, but he is a decent guy. Mix that with the tattoos and toned body, tousled hair and flippin' steel-grey eyes, and I may have to weld myself a chastity belt to keep myself under control around him.

He looks no less tasty when he looks up from the mammoth sitting next to him and sails a panty-melting smile to me. No freaking fair. How does a woman even begin to maintain herself when a guy does that? I could take up residence in his adorable dimples when his hair sweeps across his brow, forcing him to run a hand through it to push it back. I have to direct my attention to something, anything else, but him.

"That thing is huge, it's going to dent your truck," I say as I adjust my ponytail. There was a shower, so I took full advantage of the camper's bathroom facilities. I'm glad he was already dressed for the day because I used every ounce of hot water.

I look up again at Casen and he begins to chuckle. "You know, I've received several compliments over the years about my size, but never has someone suggested he would dent metal. I'm not sure what to say other than thank you."

"Oh my God, you are such an adolescent. I was talking about your dog, but I'm glad to know you pride yourself on the size of your genitalia to such an extreme." I roll my eyes and begin to walk toward the truck.

"What man doesn't value his junk, sweetheart?" he laughs. "I knew you were talking about Henri, I just like watching you squirm," he adds, hopping off the tailgate and moving around to the passenger door.

"Yeah right, whatever you say."

Casen opens the door allowing the dog to jump in and then holds it open for me. "Climb in, Jen. We need to get moving if we want to have dinner tonight."

I slide in onto the smooth leather of the bucket seat and push the horse over a bit to give myself a little more room, as it apparently has some kind of drooling condition.

"Are we going to a grocery store for food or something?" I ask once Casen is behind the wheel.

"Nope, we have to catch our dinner. We're going to Skagway Reservoir to go fishing," he answers, turning the key in the ignition, revving the engine to life.

"Um, you did hear me say I've never been camping, right? If you are depending on my fishing capability for survival, then be prepared to starve. That is, unless you want to eat your dog."

Casen pats the dog's head. Damn, I need to pay attention and remember his stupid dog's name. "Henri is the laziest, snuggliest dog on the planet. I don't think he would be very tasty."

Henri, Henri, Henri. Must. Remember. Dog's. Name. Is. Henri.

"You'll be fine, Jen. Between the two of us, we'll catch enough fish, and if not, we can always eat the hotdogs and marshmallows I have stockpiled in the camper."

"Surely there is something more valuable we can do with our day than spending it drowning worms. I'm good with hotdogs and marshmallows for tonight," I say as convincingly as possible. Casen rolls his eyes, almost ignoring my attempt to wiggle out of this fishing excursion.

Realizing this is happening whether I like it or not, I focus my attention on the scenery around us as we climb the mountain toward the reservoir. Things are blooming and it appears to be warming up, but looks are definitely deceiving. Even in this oversized sweatshirt, which by the way screams tourist due to its large printed lettering, which has 'I did 9,500 ft. at Cripple Creek' splayed across the front, I have frozen my ass off all morning. Surprisingly, the rest of the ensemble Casen picked out fits well, even the tennis shoes.

There are constant winding curves leading us to our destination. As I notice Henri encroaching on my area and the amount of drool multiplies, I become increasingly concerned with his potential motion sickness and the well-being of the limited clothing I currently possess.

"Um, is your dog going to get sick?" I ask, lifting Henri's head from my lap and moving closer to the door and away from possible disaster. Casen looks him over for a second and pats his head again.

"Nope, he's good. I think he just likes you and wants to give you a little love." He turns his attention back to the road and places both hands on the steering wheel.

I examine Henri further, not yet convinced my Walmart jeans aren't about to get sprayed with munched up kibble. I run my hand across his neck and pat his side. I have no idea what I'm looking for, but I'm hoping for some blaring sign to duck for cover, since the slobber is his apparent regular behavior. He takes this as a sign to "love" further, moving onto my lap and licking me. Now I'm concerned for my own puking status as well as my ability to breathe. "Oh sweet baby Jesus, make him not like me, make him not like me!" I squeeze out through strained breaths as I attempt to push his massive body off mine.

"Hendrix, come here," Casen bites through laughter. "Leave her alone." The horse whimpers but doesn't budge. Casen pulls the truck over and grabs his collar to pull him off me. A rush of air expands my lungs and I begin to gain feeling in my legs again. However, my ribs may never recover.

"Holy fucking shit," I pant, wiping the string of drool off my clothes. "Animals like him belong in the zoo or circus or something, he nearly killed me. I saw the white light and everything." Casen meets my agitation with even more laughter, so I turn my wrath at the elephant dog, Hendrix.

"You," I say, pointing my finger at him. "This is my space; you stay in your space. Unless you want to be our dinner alternative, keep your paws and drool out of my space."

Casen only laughs harder at my mini-overreaction to my near death experience, giving Henri the pass to bark and then lick me again across the cheek. I might have to hire someone, but this dog will possibly meet his untimely demise.

"Jen, Henri has travelled this road about a million times and he has never gotten sick. Really, he just likes you and is trying to snuggle on you. If you started to turn blue or appear as though you had internal bleeding, I would have intervened. His small bit of slobber will not kill you, I swear."

"'Small bit'? I have enough drool pooled on my jeans to alleviate the drought in all of southeast Colorado."

He laughs even harder, grabbing at his side. "Stop, no more. I can't breathe."

"Well, I'm glad. Karma is a bitch, and she always repays her debts. Maybe you shouldn't laugh at someone who is in obvious distress." I cross my arms across my chest, showing my disapproval for his lack of compassion for my unpleasant situation.

A horn honks behind us. With the narrowness of the dirt road, there is nowhere to safely pass anyone. Casen politely waves to the car behind us and puts the truck back into drive to continue on to the lake.

"You need to lighten up, Jen. If you think drool is bad, you have about ten minutes to get over it before you experience a whole new realm of ickiness. Smelly water, worms along with other various bait, and ultimately fish guts await you. So, suck it up and give in to the fact you will get dirty, wet, and smelly today. I promise you will survive it all, and maybe even have a little fun, too."

"Fine," I sigh, directing my attention back to my outdoor surroundings. It isn't long before we reach the final bend, which opens to the massive lake. The sight of the glistening water is breathtaking, and this time Hendrix has nothing to do with it. It seems so peaceful, with rows of trees, which surround the water. There is no large parking lot or beach, no expansive boat dock with lines of people waiting to launch their watercrafts. There are very few people in general; it feels like a private lake. A place to call our own, an escape from all the shit, which awaits me back home. I now understand the appeal.

"Wow," I exhale.

"I told ya," he responds with a sly smile as he parks and jumps out to gather the fishing gear from the bed of the truck. Of course, Henri stays behind, waiting on me to get out as well. It appears I won't be getting rid of my new furry friend anytime soon.

"Come on, Hulk, let's go get our fishin' on," I tell Henri and open the passenger door to step out. I exit and Henri follows right behind me. The grass is tall and reaches high up on my pant legs, the moisture leaving wet streaks on the fabric. The air is cool, but not cold enough to complain about; I'm actually comfortable and can't think of a single thing to complain about.

"The grass is somewhat high and it's getting warm; make sure you watch for snakes," Casen yells out as he heads toward the shore.

The only thing that registers is the word snake, and without thinking of following any instructions concerning them, I take off running as fast as I can toward Casen. I may come off as a tough girl, but snakes are my ultimate weakness. I can't even see those things on TV without having to change the channel. To say they give me the heebie-jeebies is putting it lightly. I refuse to even buy snakeskin boots or a purse despite their fashionable appeal. In my opinion, those creatures were put on Earth to serve only one purpose, to scare the shit out of me. May they all be bludgeoned with shovels.

Casen turns around to witness my desperate melee of wild banshee running and screaming; Henri follows behind barking loudly to match my shrieks. I see Casen's mouth moving and a stern look form on his face, but I can't make out what he's saying over the noises I'm making. As soon as I reach him, I jump into his arms and climb his body until I can wrap my legs around his waist.

"Save me, the snakes are going to eat me!" I plead.

"Shush, you're scaring the fish," he commands, gripping onto me. "Now, did you see a snake?" he asks, allowing me to remain wrapped around him.

"Well, um, no," I say after a long pause. I'm enjoying the comfort and strength of his arms which shield me from my embarrassment which will no doubt ensue once my feet hit the ground. "I heard snake and went running. You can't say things like that and not expect a woman to react drastically."

"Good to know," he laughs. "I'll keep that in mind in the future; no snakes allowed. I'm glad you're safe."

We continue to tangle around each other, ignoring Hendrix, who is circling impatiently around us. I'm not the type of girl who needs protection and affection from a man. Usually if I need something, I take it from them, but things feel different with Casen. His arms feel safe, he feels safe. It's a strange, overwhelming feeling for me. I don't let men in, but I'm sensing neither of us wants to let go.

"I'm not sure we'll catch any fish, sparky, but do you want to try anyways?" he whispers in my ear. His breath is warm on my neck and sends shivers down my body. His questions feel like more than a simple inquiry about fishing. Maybe I want him to be asking me more than about fishing. I want to be strong enough to answer both, but I don't know if I am. I've never needed a knight in shining armor, I've never wanted one. Casen, though, makes me want something I've never had…a relationship, prince and all. Instead of telling him all this, I choose the coward's path and merely nod into his neck.

Slowly, he finally releases me, allowing my body to slide down his. I notice every one of his taut muscles on my way down, and I enjoy the sensation it delivers to my system. This man is doing wicked things to me, and I don't know if I can resist the temptation much longer. He has been dangling himself in front of me since the night in the parking lot of the brewery, but has resisted any of my reciprocated flirtations. He insists it would make the tour uncomfortable and unprofessional if we dove into any kind of relationship, even if it was purely physical. I'm sure he's right, but damn he makes it hard. Even after the tour is over, I'm not sure I can let myself explore those options. Besides the physical attraction I know we share, I'm afraid of the things he would do to my heart if I let him in…a heart I have never allowed anyone to even come close to.

"Come on, sparkplug, let's see what kind of trouble we can get into," he says as he guides my feet to the ground. He grabs the fishing poles and tackle box he dropped when I mauled him and turns to find the perfect fishing spot, leaving me awestruck once again.

It's not until I register Hendrix gnawing on my sweatshirt, pulling me in the direction of Casen that I snap out of my daydream. "Stop it, Gigantor," I tell him, lightly swatting at him and pushing him away from chewing on my shirt. "You know, I think we would get along better if you didn't like me so much. The feeling isn't exactly mutual," I add.

I quickly catch up to Casen and reach him just as he begins to impale a worm with the hook on the end of his fishing line. "That is so fucking disgusting, I thought we were using bait," I say as he casts the line out into the lake.

"This is bait, Jen. I brought lots of different kinds; I just thought we would start with worms." He turns his attention to me, no doubt noticing the repulsed look on my face. "Oh, come on. It's not that bad. Just wait until you gut the fish we catch, then I'll let you complain." He chuckles to himself and wedges the pole between some rocks before picking up the other pole to hand to me. "Here, let's get your pole situated and then we can relax a little."

Gathering my courage, I pick up the small, plastic container of the slimy little creatures, but immediately my stomach twists and turns at the sight of them weaving around each other. They continue their attempt to burrow into their artificial environment; it's like they sense any second I'll select one of them to sacrifice to the fishing gods. Unfortunately, none jump out to offer themselves as tribute so I close my eyes, take a deep breath, and shove my hand into the container. I want to wuss out. I want to throw the container of worms in the dirt and tell Casen to go fuck himself. I can feel his eyes on me, and I know he's silently daring me to do just that. I refuse to lose this game.

"I can do this. I can do this," I quietly mumble to myself as the slippery little things slither around my fingers. As quickly as I can, I pull out the plump winner and brush off the stragglers, which have stuck to my hand. "Here, stick him on the hook," I tell Casen, shoving my wormy hand in his face.

"You're doing a fine job, go ahead and stick him on," he says, earning him the crustiest expression I can muster.

"You're an ass," I announce as I swipe the pole from his hands. I thought my worm selection would be enough for him, but apparently, I have to completely backwoods it to earn my Boy Scout badge. Squeezing the fishing pole between my knees to hold it still, I carefully grab the line and hold the hook as steady as possible. Casen obviously thinks I'm some rich priss who can't hold her own. I see this as the best opportunity to show him he's dead wrong about me.

I've never needed anyone's approval, never, but for some reason I can't explain, I desperately want Casen to see me as something special. I want him to want me, not because I may be an attractive challenge or because he thinks I have mad naked-time skills, but because he sees me as a beautiful seashell in a beach full of rocks. Something he wants to put in his pocket and hold dear. I'm not sure where these touchy-feely inclinations are coming from, but they're starting to piss me off.

"I can do it, Jen," Casen says reaching for the pole. "If you hold that worm any longer, I'm afraid you're going to name it and take it home as a pet," he jests, noticing my delay and reaching further for the hook.

I immediately pull away from him. "Back off, Captain America. I was just deciding how to jab him so he'll stay on the hook," I lie. Casen holds his hands in surrender and backs away to provide the space I need for this disgustingly monumental task.

It's like threading a needle, I tell myself. This little guy will net me a big honkin' fish which will be way better than anything Casen can even attempt to catch. Once my mind turns this obstacle into a competitive challenge, my rolling stomach settles and I'm able to focus. Squeezing the meatiest part I can find on him, I follow through with guiding the hook through his wiggly body. I almost dry heave, almost…my pride holds it at bay, but just barely.

Casen slaps me on the back laughing at my gusto. "Well done, sparky. I wasn't sure if you had it in you." He takes the rod from me, casts it into the water along with his, and lays a blanket on the shoreline for us to sit on as we wait for dinner to come to us.

"Yeah, well, when my Maximus the Mighty brings in the bigger fish today, you'll be sorry you ever doubted me," I explain as I take a seat on the quilted blanket. Henri lies down next to me, resting his head so close I can feel his hot breath on my leg.

"I knew you would name that worm," Casen chuckles as he sits down.

"I thought if he was going to be executed by racking and eaten by the largest fish in this lake, I should at least give him a name. Maximus seemed like the perfect name for a fishing champion." I straighten my back as I explain my path to victory, which rests solely on my selection of a creepy crawly from a plastic container.

"If we are going to make this a competition, I think a friendly wager is in order," he suggests, a smug smile gracing his beautiful face.

I'm used to "friendly wagers" with men; they usually end with someone naked and thoroughly satisfied. In fact, I'm usually the one who extends the challenge. This bet feels different though. By accepting, I may lose more than my panties, and I'm not sure I'm willing to risk more than my current Hanes Her Way specials. As safe as I feel with Casen, there is danger there. He has the power to be everything I never thought I would want, as well as the power to crush what's left of me. To let him in would be risking myself. The opportunity to drown in him is enticing, though. As carefree as he comes off, I know there is more there. He's hiding just as much as I am.

"What are you suggesting?" I ask, offering a hint of a smile.

"I want a story," he leans into me and whispers.

"A story? Like Goldilocks and shit? You don't have to catch a fish to get my best fairy tale rendition," I laugh.

"I'm thinking more of a Grimm's fairytale, but yes, a story. I'll offer up the same. I'm sure you're curious about me."

I look at the tattoos, which cascade down his arms, and I realize I, too, am curious about his past. I know more than anyone does how ink tells a story. I have a feeling his conceals his past, and revealing mine would be worth the trade.

"You've got a deal," I tell him somewhat skeptically, holding out my hand to seal the deal.

He takes my hand in his, and I feel the calluses from his profession. "Prepare to give me everything," he murmurs, pulling me close to him.

I've been fighting to stay under control around this man for the past few months. In this moment as his fluttering of words send shockwaves to my system, I know I'm prepared to give him exactly what he asks for…everything.

CASEN

"I don't know how, but I think you cheated," Jen pouts as she plops onto the log in front of the campfire. "There's no way my worm should have lost to those gross smelling salmon eggs."

"Jen, I've been fishing since I was a kid. Your worms didn't stand a chance. Why do you think I gave them to you to use?" I laugh, but she sees no humor in the situation. She pats Henri on the head to seek comfort for her loss, and dammit if he doesn't curl up next to her and nudge into her side, the traitor.

I take the foil-wrapped fish from the fire and lay them out on the picnic table to cool. I'll give Jen credit; she did catch a fish...a single fish. I, however, caught more than enough for both of us and extras to freeze and bring home. I would think she would be pleased with herself that she caught the large rainbow trout and even handled getting the hook out and gutting it herself. She, of course, had some instruction and I thought she was going to throw up on me during the process, but she managed. I was impressed. Her competitive nature has now taken over and she is pissed she lost the bet. Little does she know I had planned on sharing things about myself anyways, to make her comfortable with the information I want from her. She's hiding from something, and I want to know what it is. I want everything from this saucy woman. Very few know about my childhood; it's not something I share willingly. Yet, if I expect her to bare herself to me, I feel the need to offer the same to her.

"You jerk, it was supposed to be a fair bet," she says, giving Hendrix even more attention. Apparently, their time together today has warmed her heart toward the giant dog she hated hours ago. This morning she was willing to eat him, and now they are best buddies.

"I think it was pretty fair, but if you think you were at such a disadvantage, how about I offer something in return? To even things up, I'll answer a few questions as well. Consider it my olive branch of peace." I know the minute I proposition her, that I have her. She can't resist having the upper hand, and I know her well enough to know she thinks by having the power to ask me questions, she is in control of the conversation. I need to offer her a major gesture. Jen is not the type of girl to win over with words; she's a woman you capture with actions.

"Peace, huh?" she asks, finally giving me her attention as I bring her a plate of fish and roasted potatoes.

"Yup, I'll give you two questions in exchange for a story," I answer, as I push Henri away and Jen accepts the dinner I've made us. Sitting next to her on the log, I take it as a good sign when she doesn't slide away from me. Instead, she does the exact opposite. She bumps my knee with her own, causing my eyes to slide to hers and a smile to spread across my face.

"Three questions," she shoots at me in an attempt to negotiate.

"One," I fire back, matching her confidence.

"Ugh, fine. Two questions for one story," she concedes, rolling her eyes and finally taking a bite of her fish.

"How about I let you ask your questions first?" I offer. She nods and focuses her eyes on the crackling fire. While she works through the mental list of things to ask, I relax and dig into my dinner. I'm expecting questions about my music, or her favorite topic of conversation, groupies, or in my case, lack thereof. She doesn't know much about me, and I doubt she's cared enough to do any of her own research on my family, so I'm not too concerned about the impending inquisition headed my way.

Jen's honey eyes, which almost glow in the firelight, move to my direction and pin me in place. Her curly hair is shiny and wild, begging for the touch of my fingers. She's lacking makeup, but she looks more beautiful than anything I've ever seen. The sight of her has convinced me a smile is the best makeup a girl could ever have. I struggle to restrain myself from pulling her to me and showering her in the kisses I've been holding back since she signed on with the tour at the brewery. Seeing me squirm in the sight of her gorgeous, mangled mess brings a smile to her face and allows her to relax enough to sit back and enjoy her meal. We both know she's bewitched me, and right now, I would gladly accept any spell on my heart she could throw at me.

Finally, she clears her throat, interrupting my intoxicating daydream. "Didn't I tell you that you shouldn't feed that dog human food?" she says, pointing her fork in the direction of my plate. Henri is licking the remaining fish and potatoes I abandoned in order to partake in my apparent daily staring quota.

"No, Hendrix. Bad dog," I say through gritted teeth. The plate is pretty well licked clean, so I lay it on the ground next to me and turn my attention back to Jen, who finds the whole situation humorous. "My dog had manners before I introduced him to you," I tell her. "You've somehow ruined my best friend."

Her hand flies to her chest and she pretends to be offended, only to immediately laugh at me. "That dog was spoiled rotten way before I got here. If anything, I've reined in his only child syndrome."

Henri whimpers and lies down near her feet. A bit of jealousy stirs within me. This girl has managed to not only steal my dog, but has me envious of him, which make me feel pathetic.

"All right, ask your damn questions so we can get this over with," I snap.

"Oh my, are you sure you don't have the only child syndrome? It looks like you're struggling with some of those sharing skills." She laughs, not taking my cue and continuing to jest at my discomfort before settling in to interrogate me. I squint my eyes at her and she finally surrenders.

"Fine. Question one," she says, squaring her shoulders at me and composing herself into a serious expression. "Why music?"

"Really? That's all you've got? Why do I want to be a musician? I figured you would come up with something better than that. You're letting me off easy." Every little boy has a relatively short list of future dream professions. That list usually includes the typical Halloween costumes: a firefighter, police officer, pro athlete; even my little brother wanted to grow up and be a dinosaur. Rock star almost always makes the top ten list, so this seems like a waste of a question.

I have two choices with this question. I could go with the in-depth answer as to why I really chose music as my outlet or I could take the easy road. I see no reason to divulge more than she's asking for. So, the easy road it is.

"Doesn't everyone like music? Rock stars are cool, and they usually do pretty well with the ladies." I inject as much arrogance as possible into my answer hoping she buys it. This is certainly a believable and typical answer, just not exactly the reason why I find safety in music.

"You're so full of shit," she chuckles. "You and I both know you don't play into the groupie game like Royce. To be honest, I think you couldn't care less if you ever made the big time. You're not a rock star," she says, using air quotes. "You're a man in love with music. I want to know the real reason why."

Of course, she calls me on my shit of an answer. I hang my head, letting the warmth of the fire absorb into my skin for a minute while gathering the words for my response. I have never shared stories from my childhood.

They aren't pretty, for one. Two, hearing things like that makes people uncomfortable. The most important reason for me is the pity. I hate seeing the look on people's faces when they find out the life I had. It makes me feel like that scared thirteen-year-old boy again and brings all of the shame rushing back. The last thing I want is to see that look on Jen's face. I've worked my entire adult life at erasing that feeling of embarrassment, and one look from her could make it all wash back over me.

Taking a deep breath, I let the oxygen invade my lungs and hope the air will transform into courage and infiltrate my soul. Jen's hand slides to mine which are clasped tightly in front of me and she gently begins to stroke my fingers.

"It's okay if you don't feel comfortable sharing with me," she whispers. I can hear the hurt in her tone, and when I finally muster the guts to look her in the eyes, the disappointment is there, too. The sadness there makes my stomach twist into knots. Those eyes make me realize I would gladly bathe in an ocean of shame than ever make this woman feel unworthy of knowing me.

"No," I quickly say, grabbing her hand when she begins to pull it away. "It's just, to understand why I love music, you have to understand my past and that's not something I'm used to sharing with people."

She looks away from me, and I feel the loss of her intense stare. "I get it, Casen. It's okay; it was a stupid bet anyways."

Letting go of her hand, I reach for her smooth, rosy cheek and gently force her attention back to me. "Jen, I'm not afraid to tell you about myself," I tell her with as much conviction as possible. "I'm afraid of what you'll think of me after you know." My voice tapers off with each word, but my hand remains on her cheek, my thumb rubbing delicately along her cheekbone.

"We all have a past, Casen," she murmurs with a light smile. "I figure it's what keeps us all on an even playing field in the present. If things haven't worked themselves out or don't seem fair, karma always has a way of collecting her debts in the future."

I let her words hang in the air for a moment, allowing her simple life philosophy to sink in before I let my story spill out. "Okay," I say with a nod. "You know I was raised by my grandmother in a trailer park in northern Colorado. You know we were poor. You don't know how I ended up there, nor how music was what kept me from going down the same path as my parents."

Jen sets her plate on the ground, her dinner forgotten. Henri gladly helps her clean the plate, but neither of us bothers to instruct him otherwise. We are both too immersed in the questions I'm willing to answer.

"My parents were not great people. My mom was an exotic dancer with a craving for heroin. The drugs ultimately claimed what little life she had. My dad, on the other hand, managed to keep himself clean in terms of drugs, but he was a brutally mean drunk. He used my mom as a meal ticket, even pimping her on the streets if need be to pay the bills and their addictions. My dad knew how to play guitar and he taught me when I was young. Not as a father son activity. No, he put me on the streets with my guitar to strum up any extra change I could."

Jen's eyes haven't moved from mine, yet thankfully they haven't filled with regret for me, either. She's listening, letting my painful past therapeutically flow from me, each word healing a little piece of my brokenness.

"Whenever things got bad," I continue, "It was the music which gave me an escape from what was going on around me. Whenever my brothers and sisters were crying, it was my music, which calmed them down. Whenever my mom didn't bring home enough cash, it was my music on the streets, which quieted my father, the beast, saving us all from hours of misery. When you asked why music, there is no simple answer. Music isn't a hobby or even a profession for me. It's much more than that. It's been my escape from the pain, safety from a damaged past, it's who I am…it's what I am."

Jen breathes out heavily, mulling over her response before reacting to my answer. My throat constricts as worry overtakes me. My fear of rejection begins to take hold. But then, she scoots closer to me, so close I'm not sure where I end and she begins. "Our pasts are not who we are, they are events which have happened to us. You're a good person and I'm proud to be sitting next to you right now. The bumpy road it took you to get here doesn't change that."

Relief floods my system as her petite hand moves up and down my arm, comforting me. Suddenly her hand settles on my arm and I instantly know question number two is coming and I know what it will be.

"Go ahead and ask question two," I tell her, beating her to it. She looks to me surprised, like I wouldn't guess what the question will be. "Go on, I know what you want to ask."

She runs her hand up and then down my arm one last time and I close my eyes to fully enjoy the feeling of her skin on mine, even though I know what it is she's exploring.

"Tell me about the tattoos," she says. "I don't need to know about the images; I want to know why you got all of them." Her resolve is beginning to fade, as she knows the answer. She wants to hear me tell the story; make it real for her.

"I told you my dad was a mean son of a bitch. He never hit my mom; he knew if he banged her up, she couldn't make him money. Instead, he came after us kids. I was the oldest, I could take more than my brothers and sisters, and so many times I would provoke him to come after me instead of them. He was always coming up with new ways to hurt us, but his favorite was putting his cigarettes out on me. I have scars all over my arms where he would burn me. They became constant reminders of what I came from. When I was old enough, I started getting tattoos to cover the scars. I wanted to be released from the horrors of my childhood."

I can see she's trying desperately to hold her emotions at bay, but even Jen isn't cold enough to be unaffected. A single tear slides down her cheek, and I quickly wipe it away with my fingertips.

"How did you get out of there?" she asks, noticing her tears and swiftly brushing the remainder away.

"In junior high I had to start changing into athletic clothes for PE, which meant no more long-sleeve shirts every day. One of my teachers saw the fresh burns and called social services. Relatives all stepped up and we all were shipped to different people. My grandmother couldn't handle taking care of the little ones so I went with her. I was thirteen and could pretty much take care of myself."

"So your dad went to jail then," she states matter-of-fact, and you would think it would be the safe assumption.

"No."

Her eyebrows pinch together, irritation and anger spread across her face.

"My mother didn't want to press charges and none of the kids were willing to testify. As long as the kids were no longer in the home with my father, they didn't pursue it further."

"That is not okay," she insists and I agree. There were no consequences; it was like I endured it all for nothing. I just had to hope life would eventually catch up to him. It eventually did.

"He got what was coming to him, it just took a while. Mom died of an overdose about a year after we all were separated. My dad fell off the deep end after that. He got himself into some bad gambling debts, and well, he double-crossed the wrong person. He disappeared and we never heard from him again, but we all knew what probably happened."

My eyes have drifted back to the flames. I'm not ready yet to see the look on Jen's face after hearing my story. Then I feel her hands once again on my arm and move across one of my scars. She brings my arm to her mouth and kisses the damaged skin. The simple act makes all the fear I had been holding onto diminish. She doesn't need to say anything. I know she accepts me, and I've never been more grateful.

We both smile and enjoy a brief moment of peace. I notice her shiver, and I stand to retrieve a blanket from the camper. A now sleeping Henri doesn't even flinch with my movements. Jen, though, looks at me questioningly.

"Stay put, I'll be right back." I grab the warmest, softest blanket I can find and wrap it around her when I return to our campfire. The embers are starting to burn down, so I add another log to the fire and stir it around to get it going again.

"I believe you owe me a story now, my dear," I tell her, as I settle down next to her once again.

She snuggles down into the red, fleece blanket and turns her body into mine. "Just any story, or do you have something in mind?" she asks.

"I have something I want to know about, but I'm not sure how you'll feel about telling me."

Jen looks both nervous and confused. She's not sure where this is going, I don't either, but my curiosity to ask is too tempting. As horrible as last night's attack was, I don't think it was the cause for Jen's restless sleep. I can't help but dig into whatever it is which plagued her dreams. There is something else below the surface, and I feel like I need to know what it is in order to protect her, to have access to her guarded heart.

"While you were asleep last night, I kept checking on you," I begin to explain. Her left brow raises in concern and I shift gears momentarily. "Not in a creepy stalker way. You had me worried, and I wanted to make sure you were okay."

87

"I had a horrible night, Casen. Did you expect me to have a glorious sleep and fairytale dreams?" she asks sarcastically, now on the defensive.

"No, but what I saw was something entirely different. The events of last night triggered something for you, something you've buried. I want to know that story."

"There's no story there," she states confidently, although her actions suggest otherwise. She will no longer look me in the eyes and her body has moved away from me, allowing an undesired space between us.

"Please don't lie to me, Jen. I offered complete honesty, even though the truth is terrifying as hell for me. Please don't play that game with me."

She still refuses to look at me, but instead of retreating and letting her disengage, I push harder. "Who is Preston? You kept shouting his name in your sleep."

Her head whips around quickly in my direction to look at me, her eyes wide. Even with the overwhelming warmth of the blanket and the fire to rosy her flesh, all color drains from her face. "What did you say?" she mutters, so low I can barely hear her.

"Preston? Is he a boyfriend, someone who hurt you, someone you lost? He means something to you, I just want to know in what way." I try to ease my tone, as I don't know if this person is a good something or bad something. Either way, I feel like I need to know this if I'm ever going to really know her.

"He's someone I wish I could forget, someone I wish I had never met," she says through gritted teeth.

"So he's a past tense?" I ask, searching for a little clarification.

"I haven't seen him in years, but what he did fucked up so much of my life, every day I battle to forget." Her lips begin to tremble, but instead of the sadness one would expect, hers is a tremble of anger.

"What happened, Jen?" I say smoothly, moving closer to her and grabbing her hand like she had previously done for me.

"He stole everything from me." Her anger flares once again. "I lost my family, my friends, and for a long time, my sanity. He's not someone I care to remember. His name is a reminder of the innocence I lost."

"Please let me in," I plead. This is her story and I won't force her to share it, but I want to be the one who gets past this barrier, this gate which has locked the real Jen away.

She takes a deep breath, and looks away from me as she begins her story. I understand the feeling; this memory is as harmful to her soul as my memories are to mine.

"It was the summer before my senior year of high school. I was so excited to be finishing up and heading off to college. I was a good kid. I never stayed out past curfew, never would have been caught in the back of some guy's car, I didn't drink. My father demanded perfection, and I made sure to live up to those expectations. When the most popular guy in school asked me to go to a party, it was a given that I would accept his invitation. I was so excited, my best friend Amber, or at least I thought she was my best friend, was excited for me even though I knew she really liked him. All the girls did."

I feel my body overheat as I recognize the direction of this story, but I try to hide my anger and disdain for this asshole who broke her.

"What did he do?" I ask as controlled as possible.

"I have no real memory of it. The doctor my aunt took me to said more than likely I'd been drugged. The only people who filled my cup that night was Preston and Amber, so you do the math. I woke up the next morning in my car with torn clothing and a horrible headache. It wasn't until a few weeks later when I truly understood what happened to me."

89

I squeeze her hand, willing her to continue. "What really happened?"

"My father was sent photographs. Horrible pictures," she mumbles, looking away and brushing a tear from her cheek. It takes her several moments to collect herself enough to continue on. I don't push, I don't encourage. I just wait. She needs to tell her story in her own time, without me forcing any more of it out of her.

"I was a good kid, Casen," she finally says. The sadness dripping from her words weaves into my soul. I can't help but want to rip out my own heart to give it to her, just to erase this pain of hers. "Those pictures changed everything. The guys' faces weren't in the shots, it was only me who could be seen. They had me laid out naked on a kitchen table, doing unimaginable things."

"Did your parents call the police and press charges?" It seems like a no-brainer type of question, but judging from her reaction to the attack at the concert, there is no simple answer with her.

"It was an election year, and the pictures were meant to scare my father away from campaigning. Instead, my father called in some favors and swept it under the rug. That also meant I needed to disappear."

All emotion has drained from her as she recounts the rest of the story as if she's detached herself from it. I can relate. Retell without reliving, it's how I survived for a long time, but it doesn't heal anything. She's avoided dealing with her parents. Just like the other night, she ran.

"Disappear?" I ask.

"I went to live with my aunt to be homeschooled my senior year and then went to college at CSU. My parents pretended like it didn't happen. Even when I tried to explain, they didn't believe anything illegal had happened to me. The only one who believed me was my Aunt Maggie. She's the only one who really cared about me. But you know what? I learned a lot about who I can depend on, and what loyalty means. Now you know why I'm such a bitch. I'd rather be safe than sorry." She shrugs like the story she just shared is not some big deal. She's distancing herself again, and it blows my freakin' mind.

"Hold on here. First of all, you're not a bitch. Difficult yes, but not a bitch. Second, Preston was one of the guys, but nothing ever happened to him? How is that okay by any stretch of the imagination? Just like the fucker from Friday night, he should be in jail." I stand from the log and pace in front of her. Henry takes notice and follows me in my continued stride. My pissed level is skyrocketing. I hate that she was hurt, but her acceptance of the lack of consequences takes my anger to a new level of rage. The system doesn't always work, but I think you have to give it a chance.

"It's not fucking okay, Casen!" she shouts, jumping up from the log, stopping me mid-pace. "I was a teenager, what was I supposed to do? I don't have any memory of what happened. I've always blamed Preston because he brought me drinks and I was in his care, so I figured he and Amber were the ones who arranged it. This is something I've tried to forget about, to move past, and you're asking me to jump right back into the pile of shit which was my adolescence. No thanks."

The heat of her anger radiates off her. More than ever, I want to tuck her into my arms and never let her go. I want to make her feel safe, make her feel loved; I want to fill the void, which I now know is there.

"I just want you to feel safe," I shout back, moving within inches of her. "I want you to know you aren't alone."

Silence hangs in the air, the sound of our breathing is all that is noticeable. Before she can reject me, I twist my fingers into her sweatshirt and pull her even closer. "I want you to know you're wanted. You're worth it."

I'm hesitant for a moment, but when I see her eyes bounce to my lips and then to my eyes again, I take it as an invitation to proceed. With as much conviction as I can, I smash my mouth onto her lips. They are as soft as I remember, but now there are remnants of salt from her tears. She opens her mouth, allowing me to explore her more fully. I grasp onto her tightly and let myself get lost in the damaged beauty of this woman.

I lift her tiny body off the ground and her hands immediately wrap around my neck as her fingers crawl into my hair. The sensation of her hands on my body electrifies me, but my mind soon takes over and I know I can't let it go any farther. This is the most inappropriate thing in the world to be doing after everything she told me. Letting it go past this kiss will make me no better than those other guys.

"I'm sorry, I shouldn't have done that," I say, dropping her back down to the ground and stepping away. Tears begin to build in her eyes. She looks confused and rejected, and I want nothing more than to get away from that look.

I step closer once more, placing my hands on either side of her face and letting my forehead rest upon hers. "I want you, Jen. More than anything, I want you to be mine. But not like this." I kiss her forehead and walk away toward the trail, which surrounds the campsite.

Walking away takes every bit of willpower I have, but I refuse to be some guy she would add to the list of douchebags who took advantage of her. I don't want to be a guy she was with one random weekend. I want to be *the guy* she's with forever.

11

JEN

Casen has been gone for hours, but I can still feel the tingle on my lips from his kiss. I kiss guys all the time. Wait, that sounds slutty. I've kissed many guys in my adult life, and never have any of them made me feel the way Casen does. A single touch from him can make every ounce of my body vibrate with anticipation.

I had hoped he would let his resolve down for just another moment to allow us to explore the flirtation we had been dancing around for months. Instead of staying put and kissing me like I wish he would have, he walked away from me, panting and restraining himself.

Henri has been my companion in the camper. The lug is starting to grow on me. I've been tossing and turning, but when I hear the sound of a guitar outside I'm roused from the surprisingly soft bed. I don't find it as comfortable as it should be without Casen in it with me. I never thought I would admit to wanting a man to stay the night with me in an emotional rather than sexual capacity. Yet, here I am, yearning for Casen in any way I can get him.

I wrap myself in the same fleece blanket from our campfire chat and follow the sound of Casen's guitar. Quickly closing the door behind me as not to let Hendrix out, I sneak down the steps in a stealth-like manner, which would rival Mission Impossible. Now wearing a grey beanie to keep warm, Casen is sitting on the same log where we had shared our most guarded secrets hours earlier. His eyes are closed, lightly gripping onto his acoustic guitar. It's the most beautiful sight; it's like he is the music, the guitar is an extension of his body. This man was born to do this.

It takes a moment to decipher the song he's playing. "Moonlight Sonata" is one of the most recognizable songs, but I've never heard it played on the guitar. I've always loved the song; its melancholy rhythm always spoke to me. It had seeped into my soul, like it was written just for me. This version, while different, is mesmerizing.

I don't want him to notice me and stop playing, so I stand as still as possible at the bottom of the stairs and listen. Closing my eyes, I let the sound envelop me, losing myself in the melody. All time is lost until I hear Casen's voice boom over the music and my eyes slide open.

"You should be sleeping," he says, propping his guitar against the log.

"I couldn't. I was lonely." I move closer to him. "That was beautiful," I add, pointing to his instrument.

"I needed to clear my head. Sorry I disturbed you."

"No, not at all," I cut him off. "I needed to hear that song tonight. I just wish you would have played it for me in there," I say suggestively, nodding in the direction of the camper. My bravery momentarily shines through as I add the last line, realizing the words may be the biggest risk of my life. I've never been more afraid of rejection than I am right now standing in front of Casen.

He rubs his hands up and down his face and then takes his beanie off and runs his fingers through his soft, messy hair. "Please don't tempt me, Jen," he whispers, focusing his eyes on the beanie he's now weaving through his fingers. "It's taking every bit of willpower I have not to carry you into that camper and do all the things I hoped of doing since I had my first taste of you."

I close the distance between us and take his chin in my hand, forcing his eyes to meet mine. "I know you think being with me right now would put you in the same category as every other guy who has hurt me, used me." I take his hand in mine, lacing our finger together. "You need to understand, though, you're not taking anything I don't want to give you."

Casen delicately kisses the back of my hand and then rests my hand against his cheek. "If we take this step, there's no going back for me. I want something real, something that is just me and you. Is that something you can give me?"

"I admit I've never had that before. Honestly, I had never met a man I wanted for longer than a night. You're different, Casen. With you, I wouldn't want anything less than everything."

I drop my hand from his and wrap the oversized blanket around both of us. All reservations he has fade from his face, and a smile, which clenches my heart, replaces the apprehension. As soon as I smile back, Casen stands and lifts me in the air to carry me back to the camper. There are no more words, just his lips on mine. I wrap my legs around his strong core and hold on to this gorgeous man.

He moves quickly as if he's afraid if he takes too much time one of us might change our mind. As soon as we're inside the camper and in the bedroom, we break apart only long enough to chase Henri out of the room. Casen sprawls me out on top of the fluffy duvet, taking a second to stare down at me. Only in a Broncos T-shirt and panties, I would think I would feel self-conscience about Casen perusing my body with his eyes like this, but I don't. I feel beautiful. No more hiding, no more avoiding my past. I thought he would run when he found out, but he knows my secret and still wants me.

Casen slides out of his shoes and crawls up the bed, eventually caging me in with his solid arms. "Do you have any idea how gorgeous you are?" he murmurs as he hovers over me.

I reach up, placing my hands on both sides of his face. "Show me," I whisper.

He offers no verbal response, only actions. His lips, his hands travel every inch, conquering and devouring my body...my heart...my soul.

I hastily strip off his clothes like a child with a present on Christmas morning, rushed and frenzied. He complies with my feverish demands, but once he's undressed he grasps my wrists and places them above my head.

"Shh," he says, burying his face into my neck. "I'm not going anywhere." He licks and kisses down my neck while his hands move slowly under my shirt. After sliding it over my head, he begins making his way to my panties. Landing soft kisses along the waistband, his hands slowly slip the thin fabric down my legs, provoking a wave of chills across my body.

I've never made love. The slow, tender, passionate act is not something I've had and I look to Casen for direction. Rough, fast, and lacking all emotion other than lust is what I'm used to. I typically dominate and take what I want. To submit to Casen, to open my Pandora's Box of emotions is frightening.

I try to calm my nerves as he kisses his way up my body, but when his mouth crashes down once again on mine any leftover fears dwindle. I wrap my legs around his strong body and allow him to melt into me. As the passion of the moment reaches a fevered pitch, my feelings for Casen overwhelm me. His arms feel like my safe haven; I've not only discovered my own heart, but I've found a home within his.

The sun has started to peek through the small camper windows, and the cool morning air is beginning to filter into the room. Now under the covers, our limbs completely tangled together, we've been shifting in and out of sleep for the last few hours. Snuggling and spooning are new to me, but in Casen's arms, I could lay in this camper forever. I'm sure food can be delivered to us; of course the girls would understand my new life of hibernation.

"Hey you," Casen says as he kisses my temple.

I simply reply with a smile and cord my fingers with his.

"You know I'm not going to be able to let you go, right? I'm in this for the long haul. Me and you, sparkplug, remember?" His voice is almost pleading, a fear of rejection similar to mine laced in his tone.

"Just me and you," I reassure him. We lie in a comfortable silence, wrapped in each other's arms until I rise up on my elbow and ask him the question I've wanted the answer to since he first called me the most annoying nickname ever given.

"I have to ask. Why in the hell do you call me sparkplug?" I inquire, lightly scratching my nails along his chest.

"Sometimes I shorten it to sparky," he replies nonchalantly.

"Exactly. Instead of something sweet like baby or kitten, nope, I get Clark Griswold's pet name. Other than that usage, every other Jack Russell Terrier in the United States is named Sparky, so I'm not exactly seeing it as a term of endearment."

"I honestly never thought about that," he chuckles, wobbling my elbow, which is resting on his chest.

"Well, those are things you have to consider," I add sarcastically.

Casen rolls onto his side, forcing me to slide off him. A mischievous smile lights up his face. "All right, can I explain?"

I nod, signaling him to continue.

"Jen, you have to understand, you are the feistiest, most stubborn, headstrong woman I've ever met. You don't take shit from anyone, especially me, and yet you are one of the most loyal people I've ever come across. I adore you for all those qualities."

"What does that have to do with—" I begin to ask, but he covers my mouth with two of his fingers, cutting me off.

"Do you know what a sparkplug is?" he asks.

"I know it belongs in a car, but other than that, no." He gives me a look of disappointment. "Don't give me that look, Casen Thompson. I'm not the type of girl who rebuilds engines; I have a triple A card for a reason."

"Never once did you strike me as the type to wield a wrench," he mocks.

"Ha ha. This better be one hell of an explanation," I warn teasingly.

"Wait a minute, what's wrong with the Griswolds?" he teases. I playfully push his shoulder, causing him to laugh.

"You're such an asshole," I tell him as I try to hide my own smile.

"I certainly am, but it's what you like about me. Now hush and let me finish."

I settle back against the pillows and wait for whatever imaginative creation Casen has concocted for my terrible nickname. I always thought he was poking fun at me when he used it.

"I enjoy cars, not the new pieces of shit made of plastic, but the classics, cars with soul. You know I treat Nelly like my own child. That pickup was nothing more than a rusted out shell of a vehicle when I bought it, and it took years to restore. There is something really cool about finding something which has been abandoned, something which was thrown away and making it shine again."

I nod in agreement. I may know jack shit about cars, but I feel the same way about my photography. I love capturing those small moments when people don't think you're watching. That's where the real beauty lies, not in anything I could ever pose.

"When I met you, you reminded me so much of Nelly."

"I reminded you of your truck? Casen, my suggestion would be to offer chocolate and back away slowly. I don't see this going anywhere complimentary, when the introduction includes you remind me of my once rusty truck I found in a junkyard. Not exactly words which will convince a girl to let you under her hood."

"You're killing me, devil woman. Let me finish," he whines before briefly burying his head in a pillow.

I quietly giggle and then nudge him up. "Sorry, I'm sure this has a fabulous ending." Yeah, that probably didn't help contradict the devil woman label. I swear I try to channel my best Mother Theresa, but all that ever comes through is something, which rivals Linda Blair. "Really, keep going. Please. I want to know where the name comes from."

Casen rolls his eyes, clearly no longer amused with my interruptions and added commentary. "Like I was saying, I kept thinking of Nelly when I was around you. It wasn't that you reminded me of the actual truck, it was something specific about the truck. I rebuilt everything, my truck was perfect, but I couldn't get the damn thing to start. I checked and double checked."

"What was wrong with it?" I ask.

His eyes slide to mine and he grins triumphantly. "The sparkplug," he announces smoothly. "It's the tiniest of parts, but if something is wrong with the sparkplug, a vehicle won't work. When I met you I realized if I let you close enough, you would be my own personal sparkplug." He grabs my hip and pulls me down to my back and hovers over me. "You're a massive personality inside this tiny little package. If I didn't have you or if something were to upset you, my own world wouldn't work the way it should. I knew you would be that important to me. Am I making better sense?"

I nod and kiss him. Just like that, I don't mind the nickname anymore. In fact, I now want to hear it more than ever. I've never been important to anyone, so for him to see something more than anyone else makes me feel both uncomfortable and special.

Before I can say anything, Casen rips the blanket off me and I yelp from the immediate chill I'm met with. "What the hell?"

"It's my turn to ask a question. One last one before we have to pack up and return to the real world." He rubs his hands down my freezing body until he reaches the tattoo on my lower hip. People say tattoos are addictive, but I only have the one and I don't see that ever changing.

"Tell me the story of this tattoo. I've seen a million and a half of those dandelion tattoos with the fuzz floating off into the breeze. This, though, is the yellow dandelion flower. I could understand a rose, or a daisy, even one of those popular lilies, but a dandelion? Most people consider it a weed, not a flower. So, I want the story," he explains while his fingers trace the outline of my small tattoo. His touch leaves a trail of warmth on my skin, and I silently beg him to continue.

"That's exactly why I got it. I like to consider myself a person who survives whatever shit pile I step in or get thrown into. I'm not some fragile thing which wilts and dies. Like you said, I'm stubborn. When I decided to get a tattoo to remind myself it's okay to be a headstrong girl who not everyone is going to like, those popular flowers wouldn't work. They all need to be taken care of; if their environment isn't ideal they can't survive." As I continue to explain I feel my throat tighten and tears begin to flood my eyes. I rarely cry. I take that back, I don't cry, but I never talk about my past either, so I guess this attack of the emotions can be expected, but I hold it together. "No, I wanted the weed," I choke out. "I wanted the plant which people try and kill year after year, yet it continues to return. Its beauty isn't in the petal. The beauty lies in its will to survive. There was never any indecision, I'm a dandelion."

I feel a tear get past my defenses and roll down my temple and into my hair. I try to pretend it didn't happen so Casen won't notice. No such luck, though. Instead of using his hands to wipe my sadness away, he turns my head toward him and kisses the path of my tear.

"You got part of your description wrong, sparky. You aren't a weed. You absolutely are a flower. You are the strongest fucking flower I've ever met." His words provoke a few more tears to fall.

Casen then shifts on top of me, and brushes my hair away from my face. "Beautiful inside and out," he whispers before kissing me and grinding his hips against mine.

When he deepens the kiss, I pull away. "I thought we needed to get ready to leave?" I ask.

"The world can wait. There is nothing outside this camper more important than who is in my arms right now."

I push him off me, straddling his waist and pinning him to the bed. I lean down as though I'm going to kiss him, but I stall just before reaching him. "Don't you forget it," I tell him with a sly smile. Casen chuckles and lifts his head to meet me in the middle. Our bodies meld together and once again passion overtakes us. He was right. The world and everything in it can wait.

CASEN

"Thank you for dinner," she says, placing the key in the lock to her apartment.

I wrap my arms around her tiny waist and smell the coconut scent of her hair. "You are very welcome." I playfully tickle her sides. "Are you inviting me in for coffee or 'coffee'?"

She laughs and opens the door. "Why don't you come on in and we'll play it by ear," she says, walking through the doorway.

I follow her into the apartment and take my boots off on the rug in the entry. Collages of black and white photography adorn every wall in her apartment. I was expecting vibrant colors, but instead the cozy one-bedroom is subtle, comfortable, and decorated in shades of light green and lavender. The flowers in the vases are fake, which is not surprising after hearing about Jen's inability to keep plants alive.

"So now that you have me here, what do you plan to do with me?" I joke as I move into the living room and take a seat on the lush cream-colored sofa. Photography books, fashion magazines, and a few pieces of mail are scattered across the dark brown coffee table, but that is the extent of the clutter in the apartment. Campbell told me about an incident in college when she and Vivian hid her favorite designer heels as a way to teach her a lesson in cleaning up after herself. I guess the girls got their message across, because her place is neat and tidy.

"I haven't figured that much out yet, I figured a movie or maybe a game. I have a closet full of board games." She throws her purse on the kitchen counter and disappears into the hallway.

"Playing cards for drinking games are kind of a given hanging out with guys, but other than poker, I haven't ever played any board games. We really didn't have those when I was a kid," I explain.

She returns to the living room with a stack of games in her hand and drops them on the floor in front of me. "Well, you have no choice now, we're playing a game. I can't let you continue on without having participated in games like Uno or Yahtzee. That's just wrong."

"Hey now, you had never been fishing or camping. I think we are pretty even," I defend myself, sorting through the game possibilities.

"Whatever. You pick something out while I get us some snacks and drinks." She stands and takes off toward the kitchen. I hear the fridge open, followed by a great deal of crashing and banging from her direction. I'm interested to see what she comes up with because I know her culinary skills are limited. Unless one counts her ability to order takeout, then she's a pro.

She returns with big bags of candy, a bowl of popcorn and cans of soda. "I have found us a feast," she says, obviously fond of her kitchen bounty. "What are we playing?"

I hold up the Yahtzee box and shake the dice inside. "It's on, woman."

Taking the red box from me, she instantly starts setting up the game on the floor and explaining the objective. By the time she's done, I'm convinced this is a game designed by elementary teachers to trick kids into learning addition. Nevertheless, the game seems pretty kickass.

"You want to go first?" I ask, shoving a handful of popcorn in my mouth. Immediately I'm thankful for her selection of extra butter as it helps to mask the burnt taste caused by her leaving the bag in the microwave a little too long. Choking down the final bite, I open my Dr. Pepper and wash down the leftover charcoal. I take a mental note to stick with the numerous bags of candy for the remainder of the evening.

"No, you go ahead," she says opening her own can, which explodes all over her. "Dammit," she shouts, attempting to shield herself from the spray of the soda. She stands up and rushes to the kitchen for a towel and I quickly move the game away from the sticky mess. Thankfully, nothing is ruined except maybe Jen's outfit.

She returns sopping wet with a tea towel and an expression, which clearly says, proceed with caution. "Time out for now, I'm going to take a shower and change into some clean clothes."

I bite back a laugh at the state of her disarray. "No problem, sparkplug, I'll catch up on my Cosmo and review my Yahtzee strategies."

She nods and storms down the hall to her bathroom. It's not until the water pipes rattle to life that I remember the length of Jen's typical showers. I may be asleep on the couch before I see her again as I'm looking at a forty-five minute to hour-long wait. To waste some time, and keep myself awake, I find tasks around the apartment to accomplish. I finish cleaning up the soda mess, throw away the ruined popcorn, making sure to make a new bowl so she won't notice my little switch, and stack the board games up. Those tasks took a total of ten minutes, only ten minutes, and the water is still going strong.

Grabbing the large photography book off the coffee table and plopping onto the couch, I hope the pictures are enough to keep me occupied for the next who knows how long. I flip through the first few pages of buildings and pasture pictures, nothing that speaks to me. I think that's the inspirational phrase used by artsy types. When I notice a bookmark holding the place of a particular picture in the middle of the book, I find myself hoping Jen has marked something spectacular which will help me justify her purchase of this ungodly expensive, and less than impressive, picture book.

Turning to the marked page, I'm immediately struck by the image on the page. The personal meaning of the photo pulls me in and I feel as though I shouldn't even be looking at the picture. The picture is meant to be a field of healthy, beautiful roses. What stands out is not the sea of red, though, it's the lone yellow dandelion which stands against the fray. A weed amongst the flowers…a dandelion amongst the roses. This picture symbolizes Jen and for a split second I contemplate ripping it from the book so I can have it all to myself.

A sense of paranoia overtakes me and I listen intently for the water, which is still running. I begin to put the bookmark back in its place, when I notice it's not a bookmark at all, it's a letter from her Aunt Maggie. I know it's an extreme invasion of privacy, but I can't help myself from wanting to look at it. The postmark is current, yet the folds of the stationary suggest this letter has been opened and closed several times…probably read many more. This letter has held the place of this picture in her book for a reason.

I slowly open the letter, careful not to rip the thinning pieces of paper. A few photos of a little girl drop out into my lap. They're the same child at different ages; the newest looks to place the girl at maybe age nine or ten. The little girl in the pictures, if she isn't Jen as a child, is definitely someone related to her. After examining each photo, I place them back in the envelope and turn my attention to the letter. I listen once more for the shower to make certain I'm safe to proceed and then dive in.

DEAR JEN,

I HOPE THIS LETTER FINDS YOU WELL, MY DEAR. IT HAS BEEN A WHILE SINCE WE LAST SPOKE, BUT I FEEL AS THOUGH THIS LETTER IS LONG OVERDUE. I WANT YOU TO KNOW I LOVE YOU LIKE YOU WERE MY OWN DAUGHTER AND EVERYTHING I'M ABOUT TO TELL YOU I DID OUT OF LOVE FOR YOU.

WHEN YOUR FATHER SENT YOU TO ME ALL THOSE YEARS AGO, I NEVER AGREED WITH WHAT HE WAS FORCING YOU TO DO. CHOICES WERE TAKEN FROM YOU, AND I JUST COULDN'T DO THAT TO YOU. YOUR FATHER GAVE ME LEGAL AUTHORITY TO HANDLE THE ADOPTION, TO DISTANCE HIMSELF FROM EVERYTHING, BUT I NEVER DID AS HE INSTRUCTED.

I FOUND YOUR DIARY AND READ ABOUT YOUR FEELINGS ABOUT THE BABY, HOW YOU WISHED YOU WERE ABLE TO KEEP HER, NO MATTER HOW SHE HAD BEEN CONCEIVED. I READ IF YOU WERE ABLE TO KEEP HER, YOU WOULD NAME HER ABBY. YOUR WORDS BROKE MY HEART. I KNEW YOU WEREN'T READY TO BE A MOTHER, AND YOUR FATHER WOULD NEVER BE ACCEPTING OF WHAT I HAD PLANNED, SO I'VE KEPT THIS SECRET ALL THIS TIME. I THINK IT'S NOW TIME YOU KNEW THE TRUTH.

I ARRANGED THE PAPERWORK AS I WAS
INSTRUCTED BY YOUR FATHER, BUT
INSTEAD OF ADOPTION PAPERS, YOU
SIGNED PAPERS GIVING ME POWER OF
ATTORNEY AND GUARDIANSHIP OF
YOUR DAUGHTER. AFTER SHE WAS
BORN, I SENT HER TO LIVE WITH
FRIENDS UNTIL YOU LEFT FOR SCHOOL.
THEN SHE CAME TO LIVE WITH ME,
WAITING FOR A TIME WHEN YOU COULD
BE HER MOTHER. I'M SO SORRY IF THIS
ISN'T WHAT YOU WANTED AND FOR NOT
TELLING YOU, BUT I DIDN'T SEE ANY
OTHER WAY OF SOMEDAY REUNITING
YOU WITH YOUR CHILD.

IF YOU'RE READY, ABBY IS READY.

WE LOVE YOU,

AUNT MAGGIE

The words of the letter punch me in the fucking gut.
How do I not bring this up, but how can I approach her
with it either? I don't think she'll act on the situation
unless she's pushed, as evident by the unanswered letter
which is falling apart. I can't let her family slip through her
fingers.

"Hey, you ready to play?" I hear Jen's voice from the
end of the hallway.

I shove the envelope and its contents back into the
book, lay it on the coffee table, and reach for the bowl of
now cold popcorn. I try to remain as unaffected as
possible, but I know if I stay I won't be able to keep
myself from asking her about it. I can't pretend I didn't
read that letter. The only person I can think to ask is
Campbell, and I have every intention of calling her

tomorrow and gathering as much information as possible about Aunt Maggie.

"Jeeeez, sparky, you were in there forever," I say with a fake yawn and a stretch. "I'm exhausted, can we just go to bed?" Standing up, I close the distance between us and pull her into my arms. I want to hug her hard enough to fix everything which is broken, give her back all that was taken from her.

"Mmm, you're not too tired are you?" she sighs, leaning into me.

I kiss her softly, letting her taste and her scent seep into my pores. Her soul crawls under my skin. "I'm never too tired to love you, sparkplug, but tonight I need to just hold you."

She smiles and entwines her hand with mine and leads me to a place my heart will never return from.

13

JEN

"I can't believe you got him that. You better hope he can take a joke," Casen says as we get out of Nelly and carry our gifts up the pathway to Brooks and Vivian's home. Every tree along the way has been attacked by pink balloons and streamers. I'm sure Grace and Emma are to blame...like Brooks needed any help going overboard with this party.

"Women get all of the presents at these things, it was only fair we bring Brooks something too," I tell him. Never mind that my gift is entirely inappropriate and will likely piss him off more than make him smile, but that's how mine and Brooks' relationship has always been. We show each other we care about each other by creatively coming up with the best way to give one another shit. I don't mean to brag, but I usually win.

"I'm glad I picked up the extra present to take the edge off the gift you're giving," he laughs as he knocks on the enormous door and we wait to be let into the party.

Blake answers the door, less than enthused. "Hey Aunt Jen, everyone is out back, just follow the pink."

"Wow, buddy, that bad huh?" I ask him, handing him a present. "This one is for you. I figured there would be enough girly stuff around for a while, you needed something manly."

He rips through the Spiderman wrapping paper revealing the Teenage Mutant Ninja Turtle action figures. "Holy crap!" he shouts, a smile finally appearing. He immediately looks around. "I mean holy cow. I'm not allowed to say crap," he explains, lowering his voice.

"Don't worry, I won't tell. Besides, crap is pretty mild in my book." I lean in, quietly reassuring him.

"Thank you, these really are cool."

"Don't thank me; I don't even know who they are. Casen picked them out." He opens his mouth to give the history of the half-shell ninjas and I hold my hand up to stop him. "I've been filled in. Casen told me all about Shredder and Splinter...the whole detailed story of the green warriors."

"I would love to take you to the turtle movie when it comes out in a few months, if you want to," Casen adds. If I thought the kid's smile couldn't have gotten any wider, I would have been wrong.

"That is so cool! Thank you," he shouts before running to his room. He's probably finding the perfect hiding spot for his warrior force before the girls get ahold of them and beautify them with a spa day or something.

As instructed, we follow the pathway of pink to the back deck. "Holy hell, it looks like a tragic Bubblicious accident!" I exclaim, opening the backdoor to the baby shower of a lifetime. Piñata storks are perched on every railing, game stations are set up around the yard, and the pile of presents could rival the year-end inventory at Toys"R"Us.

Vivian stands from her throne of presents and rushes to us, pulling us both into a warm embrace. "I'm so glad you both came," she says for all to hear. Then she pulls us closer to whisper in our ears, "Brooks and the girls went a little crazy, please play nice."

I'm prepared to tell her best of luck with that, when Casen speaks over me. "I'll keep her reined in as best I can, Vivian."

Vivian pulls away with a stunned look, which matches my own. "Oh hell, I never thought I would hear a man say that about her. If you're going to attempt to rein her in, you better hang on tight; you're in for quite a ride," Vivian laughs loudly.

"I'm so glad you both can laugh at my expense. Payback is a bitch, just remember that," I huff and walk away to add my presents to the Mt. Everest of wrapping paper.

Finding a seat closest to the My Little Pony inflatable scene, I only have seconds before I'm bombarded with the Emma and Grace duo. They're covered in sparkles, topping off their ensembles are tiaras and feather boas, too.

"Aunt Jen, we're going to smell and eat baby poop, you want to be on our team?" Emma asks.

"Yeah, my daddy says you're good at eating poopy," Grace adds.

I now have absolutely no regrets giving Brooks my present, but instead of saying anything about him, I merely smile at the girls. Casen sits down next to me, stifling a laugh and I shoot him my best death glare. He holds his hands up in surrender and turns his attention to the girls.

"So, you girls are going to play the smell the diaper game?" he asks them. "We would love to be on your team as long as you'll share some girly party accessories with us. I think we need to match as a team, don't you?"

Apparently he didn't understand the meaning behind the death glare, so I hit him with it again. This time, he ignores the threat. The girls jump up and down and race inside to grab their best dress-up items to prepare us for the baby shower Olympics.

"Oh, lighten up," he says once the girls are inside. "I would think playing dress-up with crowns and jewels would be your thing."

"You know, your priority shouldn't be getting the kids to like you, it's supposed to be getting me to like you," I tell him.

"I'm not too worried, you already like me," he gloats, easing back in his chair and resting his arm on an inflatable.

"It will be worth it to see you dressed in feathers and makeup. Today we are going to test the boundaries of your masculinity."

"Well, in that case, I'm going to seek out the other men folk and bulk up on testosterone before the bite-sized glitter girls wage siege on my manhood." He kisses me and squeezes my thigh before leaving me alone to find Brooks and Brooks' brother, Lakin.

The guys have folded Casen into the crew seamlessly. Everyone gets along and it feels like he's one of us, not someone who's casually stopping through, but actually belongs here. I can't help but stare at him interacting with the other guys. I never would have thought I would be in this comfortable situation with a man, but surprisingly, I'm thankful it's happened.

"He seems like a great guy," Carly says, interrupting my stalker session and sitting down in Casen's vacated seat.

"Who would have thought I would find someone willing to put up with my shit, and I would wait around long enough to let them," I tell her with a smile.

She laughs, but it's not the sincere giggle Carly is known for. There's a sadness which surrounds her. I may be the bitch of the group, but I won't ignore when something is bothering her. I'm sure being here around all of this baby mania after all the trouble she and Jack have had only adds to it.

"Where's Jack?" I ask, noticing he's not circling the grill with the rest of the guys.

"He couldn't come," she says, looking away from me. "He had to work."

"On a Saturday? What in the hell's going on, Carly?"

She takes a moment before responding. "I don't know, Jen," she finally says, turning to look at me. "Things haven't been okay for a while. I don't know what to do anymore." Her watery eyes show the pain of the situation and I feel helpless to make it better for her.

I grab her hand and squeeze tightly. "Is it the baby thing, or is there something else going on?" I ask.

"You know, that's what I thought the tension was stemming from, but I'm not so sure anymore. Jack won't talk to me and he's not home much."

I realize what she's implying and if it's true, heaven help Jack. He won't only need a good divorce attorney, he'll need a bodyguard for the hit I'll have taken out against him.

"Jack's not stupid enough to think he could get away with something like that," I insist.

"Maybe he doesn't care if he gets caught," she replies with a quiver of her lip. Someone catches her eye and she instantly changes her demeanor. I follow her line of sight and see Vivian and Campbell are headed in our direction, full of smiles and plates full of food.

"I don't know what you two are gossiping about, but it's present time. Get your asses in position for baby overload," Campbell jests.

Vivian and Brooks find comfortable spots and begin ripping through the mountain of diapers, onesies, and receiving blankets.

"This one is from me," I tell Brooks, sliding my special gift toward him. "And this little one is from Casen, he insists they go together," I add.

His brows scrunch together, unsure of whether or not to risk public humiliation by opening his gift in front of everyone.

"Just open it," I tell him when he continues to hesitate.

Slowly peeling away the blue wrapping paper, Vivian's lips curl around her teeth, attempting to hold in her laugh when the gift is revealed. He looks to me for an explanation I'm surprised he needs.

"Vivian told us how you're taking the plunge and getting the man marbles snipped. I thought a plastic dog cone would be a useful gift for your impending procedure. I had to go to three different vet clinics to find it."

He pulls out the oven mitts with pictures of puppies on them and looks questioningly at me. "To keep your hands away from your battle wounds. Viv doesn't need you scratching and popping a stitch."

Our friends burst into laughter, although Brooks looks less than enthusiastic. "You're time is coming, MacLauchlan, and I will be there waiting to embarrass the shit out of you," he promises.

"Here, man. This might be a little more useful," Casen tells him, handing him our smaller gift.

He shows less apprehension towards Casen's gift, tearing it open. With a massive grin, he exposes the bottle of whisky. "Now that's a useful gift!" he says excitedly. "Come on boys, these ladies can handle the rest of the gifts. Let's go crack this baby open."

Lakin and Casen follow Brooks into the house in search of glasses. "The games will start soon and I'll be taking pictures, boys. Drunk or not, I expect a picture with your new gifts, Brooks," I call after them.

As the glass doors open, laughter erupts at the sight of the guys. Emma and Grace, along with the little mini-tag-a-long, Olivia, lead the pack of fluffed and feathered, jeweled and manicured. We thought the men had gotten lost in sports conversations and booze. Apparently eye shadow and nail polish found them instead. I grab my camera and begin taking snapshots of the princess brigade.

"Aren't they pretty?" Emma asks.

"Oh, they are gorgeous, cricket!" Vivian exclaims.

"Daddy said he wouldn't dress up unless he got the purple boa. He said it looks the best with his dark hair," Grace adds.

Brooks rolls his eyes and then twirls the feathers. "It brings out the blue in my eyes," he says in a high-pitched tone.

"Your daddy always has been a bit of a diva," Campbell says laughing. "But Casen and Lakin, what's your excuse?"

"I wanted them to like me, and he was feeling left out," Casen says pointing to Lakin.

"Hey now, I'm the cool uncle, I couldn't leave my girls hanging. I'm manly, thank you very much; I do Kung Fu." Lakin tries to plead his case, but fails miserably in his aqua-toned makeup and red-jeweled tiara.

"Whatever gets you through, Nancy," I tell him as I click the camera.

"Hey there, sparkplug, any of these pictures end up on the tour flyers and there will be retribution," Casen threatens. "There are still a few more shows left and we do want a record deal when it's over."

"Don't worry, your secret is safe with us," Carly chimes in.

"Are we playing games or wh—" Blake begins to say as he exits the house and sees the guys in their princess outfits. He closely examines each one of them with a look of bewilderment smeared across his face.

"Does this make me the man of the house, Mom?" he asks Vivian. She laughs instead of answering him. He then sizes up Casen again before addressing him individually. "I'm pretty sure the turtles don't wear makeup. If you guys need to remember how to be guys, I guess I could play action figures with you."

"All right, enough. Let's get these games going," Brooks interjects. "What are the teams?"

"I would say boys versus girls, but I don't think I can take on everyone by myself," Blake explains, prompting the men to share a look of insult.

"How about us women versus you girls? Blake, you can be the referee," Campbell suggests.

Everyone agrees and heads down the stairs of the deck to the games set up on the lawn. Baby trivia, baby food in a diaper guessing game, changing and dressing the baby partner challenge; the men kicked our asses at each one. Well, Brooks and Lakin weren't much help to their success, but between the girls' small hands and Casen's experience with his younger siblings, they destroyed us. The men took their victory lap carrying the girls on their shoulders around the yard while we pouted. Campbell and I weren't expected to be much help. Hell, I killed a Chia Pet once. Vivian and Carly are moms, though. I'm going to blame nerves and intimidation, I may even stoop low enough to declare the men cheated, but either way, it was a pathetic showing on our part.

"You just earned diaper duty for the first two months, sweetheart," Vivian teases Brooks.

"And you lost naked time privileges for the next month, big guy," I tell Casen. "Vivian is kidding, I'm not."

He wraps his arms around me, smearing his makeup on me. "We both know you can't go that long, sparky" he whispers.

I push him away lightly, "You don't want to challenge me, Mr. Thompson. I have enough electronic love machines to put the Shop Erotic show off the air and out of business." I know he's absolutely correct, but I'm also a sore loser.

"Here, let me help you with your celibacy mission," he says before turning to the rest of the group and clicking his glass to gain their attention. "Jen and I have one last gift for you. We thought you guys might need a weekend away before the baby comes so we would like to watch the kids for you."

Mouths drop open in disbelief, including my own. He continues with his offer, though. "We thought we could take all the kids camping up at my regular camping spot outside Colorado Springs. Fishing, hiking, s'mores, the kids will love it. Carly, we would love to have Olivia come along as well."

I love all the "we" shit he's throwing out there. Everyone looks to me for my approval of "our" offer. The girls know I'm the farthest thing from maternal, and me babysitting for an hour is a stretch, let alone an entire weekend. They do value their kids, and placing them in my care is probably a scary notion.

"Wow! That would be amazing!" Vivian screeches.

"I would owe you so big, man!" Brooks says at the same time.

Apparently they are more desperate for a weekend together than I thought. I look to Carly, my voice of reason. "Well, if everyone is on board, then I'm okay with it. Are you sure about this, Jen?" she asks.

Shit, I'm backed into the "we" corner. I have no choice but to agree, or I come off as the asshole who doesn't want to help out friends.

"Of course! There's a Walmart a few miles away where we can get the fishing gear and anything else we need, the camper is great, and the hiking trails are wonderful. The kids will have a blast; there's nothing to worry about."

Eyes wide, everyone's attention is now on me. I thought I was pretty convincing.

"You went to a Walmart? Casen, what did you do to our friend? She wouldn't have been caught dead in a Walmart," Brooks says.

"Oh, screw you guys, you want the gift or not?" I shoot back.

"There she is," Vivian laughs. "Yes, we accept your gift, thank you."

Smiling, I turn to Casen and silently mouth the only words, which come to mind, "We're fucked." He laughs, but I'm entirely serious.

CASEN

"Dude, that was fucking epic," Seiger yells, running off stage. "This was the best show of the tour."

I couldn't disagree. We played our hearts out tonight, thank God. Campbell didn't tell the other guys, but there were record label representatives in the audience tonight. My stomach has been in knots all evening, but not because of our chance at a record deal. My anxiety stems from the extra guests I've invited to the show who are waiting for me in the dressing room. Campbell got me the number I needed and slipped them backstage, but she did so with a cautionary warning. My plan could blow up in my face, but I just couldn't leave it alone.

Sweat is dripping off all of us; John looks like he walked through a car wash. That doesn't stop Jen from taking pictures of us, though. Campbell meets us off stage with towels and a giant smile. She is absolutely dressed for the occasion. Her hair is pinned up in a sleek rockabilly hairdo, which matches her form-fitting dress and patent-leather heels. We're all careful not to get her pristine outfit wet.

"I've some great news for you, boys," she announces. "I have a meeting set up for you tomorrow with a rep from Sony Records. Congratulations, guys, they're prepared to offer you a record deal!"

"Fuck yeah they are," Royce shouts, high-fiving Seiger.

John picks up Campbell, disregarding his sweat, odor, and her outfit, and swings her around, landing a sloppy kiss on her cheek. "We owe you so big, Cam."

"Don't thank me. You guys play the music they like, I just got them to the show," she laughs, taking the towel from John and drying herself off.

Jen hangs back away from our celebration, capturing the moment on film. Grabbing her hand, I pull her into the excitement. "I want to share this with you, sparky. This is something I've always wanted, and you're helping to complete the other missing piece," I tell her, adding a chaste kiss which makes her giggle.

"And what would that be?" she questions.

"A family," I murmur in her ear. She smiles so bright and luminous it melts me. I want nothing more than to look at her smile every day for the rest of my life. I only hope I still get the chance after Jen finds out what I've done.

"Let's go celebrate! Beers on me tonight," Royce shouts, earning cheers from everyone.

"Thanks, man, but I have some people waiting for me," I tell him, declining his offer. Jen looks at me confused and I give her a reassuring smile. I glance over at Campbell and her tight-lipped smile does nothing to ease my nerves. I have never been so unsure of anything in my life.

"I'm going to stay behind and finish some things here. Text me where you guys decide to go and I'll meet you there," she tells Royce. I know she has nothing to finish. She's staying for moral support in case my plan goes south. Whether she's there to comfort me or calm Jen, I don't know. Either way, I'm glad she's willing to stick around.

They agree and head out the backdoor, leaving Campbell, Jen, and me alone. "I'll be around, Casen, if you need anything," Campbell offers and returns to the front of the bar.

"I'm starting to feel uneasy, Casen. What in the hell is going on?" Jen asks. She's looking around, searching for clues as to what I have in store.

I grab her hand, weaving her fingers in mine and kiss her knuckles before tucking them into my chest. "I need you to follow me, but first I need to tell you something."

"You're freaking me out. What in the hell is going on?" She takes a step away from me, but I pull her back into my embrace.

"I want you to know I love you, and what I've done, I did because I love you. I know this is the first time I've told you that, but I do. I love you, and I need you to hear it and believe it."

She reaches up and lightly brushes her hand against my cheek. I close my eyes and lean into her hand, memorizing her touch. "I love you too, Casen. Now tell me what you did." Noticing my distress, her voice is soft and comforting.

"I made some phone calls and invited some people to meet us tonight. I didn't think you would ever do this on your own, so I'm giving you the nudge I think you need. They're in the dressing room waiting for you. If you want, I can go in with you, or I can wait out here. I'll do whatever you ask."

Her brows pull together briefly before she yanks her hand from mine and storms off down the hall toward the dressing room. She stops in front of the door and pauses with her hand on the doorknob. She looks at me one last time, before twisting the knob and pushing the door open. Standing in the doorway, frozen in place, she stares at Maggie and Abby who are waiting on the other side of the doorway.

She closes the door and hastily returns to me. "Leave," she demands. She is shaking and on the verge of tears. The last thing I want to do is leave her when she's like this, especially because my actions caused this.

"Jen, please—" I begin to plead, but her shout interrupts me.

"I said leave," she screams, her tiny hands finding strength in her rage to push me away. "How dare you go behind my back and do this. Seeing them was my decision, not yours."

Her anger radiates off her and I realize nothing I say will tear down her wrath right now. The best I can do is respect her wishes at the moment, and hope she forgives me later.

"I'm sorry, Jen. I just thought this reunion wouldn't have happened without a little help. I thought I was doing the right thing."

"Maybe it wouldn't have, but it was my choice to make," she sighs, tears filling her eyes. "Please, Casen. Just go. I can't do this right now." She looks down at the floor, unable to look at me anymore, leaving me nothing left to do except leave.

I kiss her head and allow my fingers to run through her silky hair. I feel her take a ragged breath under my hand, and it rips my heart from my chest.

"Please," she whispers.

I nod and walk out the backdoor; leaving my heart behind, I hope it makes its way back to me.

JEN

My legs won't move. I'm torn between running out to the parking lot and getting as far away as possible, and going back to the dressing room to meet the daughter who was taken from me, the person I didn't think I deserved.

I've held onto my aunt's letter for a month, trying to decide what to do. Eventually I would have reached out to them, but when I first read it, and every time since, I'm overwhelmed with anxiety. I'm conflicted with a number of intimidating thoughts: Fear of rejection, fear of having to explain where I've been and why I haven't been in her life, fear of telling her how she came to be. Talking about those things makes them real, and for the last decade I've done a great job of avoiding it all. When I left my aunt's home I shoved all those cruel memories deep down, hoping that they would never resurface. It wasn't until Casen that I was forced to face my hurtful past. Now, my previous life is sitting on the other side of the door waiting for me.

Gathering every bit of courage I can find, I slowly take the twenty steps to the dressing room door. Before I can change my mind, I turn the knob and open the door. Taking the first step into the room, I let fate take over from there.

"Hi, sweetheart," my aunt says, rushing to me and pulling me into her arms. "I'm so glad you came back."

"I just needed a minute, but I'm ready now," I tell her quietly. "Does she know about me?" I ask her, afraid of what the answer might be.

"Jen, honey, she knows everything. She is so excited to meet you." Her reassurance provides so much relief. The knot in my stomach loosens and for once, I think I can actually go through with this.

Maggie takes my hand and guides me to the couch, where my daughter is patiently yet nervously waiting for me. It's amazing how much she looks like me. Her brown eyes and blonde hair remind me of myself at her age and I'm overwhelmed with grief for all the things in her life I missed out on. First steps, first words, first day of school. I missed it all. I'm jealous of my aunt's involvement in Abby's life, and simultaneously I'm thankful that she cared enough to do what she did for me.

Maggie lightly grabs Abby's hand and pulls her up from the couch so we're face-to-face. "Jen, this is your daughter Abby. Abby, sweetheart, this is your mom."

Maggie's introduction was so simple, yet her words hit me like a giant freaking boulder. I'm a mom. I never let myself even consider the words before, because the label was taken from me. But Maggie has given it back to me. I'm Abby's mom and I've never wanted anything more.

I reach out my hand to shake hers, unsure of what the situation calls for. I want to hug her, I want to tell her I'm sorry this happened to us. Yet I don't know where the boundaries are and I don't want to mess this up. Instead of the momma bear hug I want to give her which would rival Vivian's, I reach my hand out like an olive branch, hoping forgiveness finds its way to the other end.

Though, instead of a hand, Abby jumps into my arms, wrapping her little arms around my waist and squeezing so hard it knocks the wind out of me. "I'm so glad you're here, Mom," Abby says excitedly.

I place my hands on her head and smooth her wild hair down with tears running down my cheeks. I take a deep breath, the strain in my throat making it difficult to breathe. "There isn't anywhere I would rather be, baby girl. I'm not going anywhere, anymore."

As angry as I was with Casen for intruding on this, now that I'm holding Abby in my arms all of my rage has disappeared. I don't know how to thank him for forcing me to take the leap I'm not sure I would have done on my own. He helped return the most valuable thing I've ever lost, and I wish he was here to be a part of the homecoming. I can never thank him enough for bringing my daughter back to me. He created a family for me, and I don't know if I'll ever be able to repay the debt.

15

JEN

"Am I understanding this correctly? Casen found your aunt's letter about the daughter you were forced to give up for adoption, who your aunt actually hid instead and he arranged a reunion for you all?" Vivian asks, throwing herself onto her plush loveseat and digging into a bag of Snickers.

I nod, insecure about my friends' reactions to my tainted past.

"And you haven't seen him since that night?" Carly adds, throwing a few Skittles into her mouth.

"He's texted me and I've texted back, but I haven't seen him. I don't know what to say. I'm thankful for what he did, but I'm embarrassed at the same time. I never told him about Abby. I've spent the last decade trying to forget she existed. I never in a million years thought I would have a chance to see her again, let alone be her mother." The entire situation has made me physically sick. This week away from him has plagued my body to the point I think I've caught the flu.

"So, is she going to come live with you? What's the plan?" Vivian asks.

I slide off of the couch onto the floor and bury my face in my hands. I'm sure I've smeared whatever makeup is left on my face. "We're taking things slow. We have some visits planned to get to know each other, and we'll take it from there," I explain.

My stomach rumbles and a wave of nausea hits me. I knew I should have stayed home; Brooks will kill me if I get his pregnant wife sick.

Vivian unwraps a Snickers and hands it to me. "Here, hun, chocolate makes everything better."

I pop the little morsel in my mouth, but the instant my taste buds recognize the velvety milk-chocolate, the slight nauseous feeling from a few minutes ago escalates which forces me to test my indoor track skills. Without a word, I stand and sprint to the bathroom to rid myself of not only the Snickers but also the few saltine crackers I had managed to keep down.

I feel a cool washcloth on the back of my neck and then a bottle of water is placed on the floor next to me. Through the haze of my misery I hear Vivian's voice, "Are you okay, hun?"

I use the cloth to wipe my neck and face before taking a drink of the cold water to calm my burning throat. "This whole situation has me so upset. I think I'm coming down with the flu."

Expecting nothing less, Vivian feels my forehead for fever. "You don't feel warm, are you sure it's the flu?" she says, helping me off the floor. She puts the toilet seat down and helps me sit down.

"Of course," I insist. "All week I've been worn down and tired and I can't keep anything down. My throat doesn't hurt so I don't think it is strep. Even the smell of my lattes make me sick, so I've had the worst caffeine headache the last few days."

Vivian begins to rummage through her medicine cabinet above the sink, and I'm hoping she finds a bucket of Pepto Bismol and a bottle of aspirin. I'm stunned with what she pulls out and places on the counter instead.

"A pregnancy test? Really, Viv? I need to rest for a few days and I'll be fine."

Vivian ignores my protest and begins unwrapping the packaging. "Jen, do you realize how many of these I've peed on? I've given birth to two babies and am pregnant with another, I think I'm familiar with the symptoms of pregnancy. Plus, I've known you long enough to know the signs of denial."

She hands me the stick and smiles gently. "Just pee on the damn stick."

I snag it from her hand with an eye roll. "Fine," I relent. "If it will make you feel better."

Vivian opens the door to give me a little privacy and as the door opens Carly and Campbell, who have apparently been eavesdropping, fall into the doorway of bathroom.

"Holy shit, Jen," Carly shouts, staring at the test in my hand.

"Sorry," Cam offers. "We just wanted to make sure you were all right."

Vivian pushes them both out of the room and begins to close the door. "We'll be right out here when you're done; I'll even have the Pepto ready for you." She closes the door and leaves me with the stick of fate.

Holding it in my hand, I mentally run through my womanly calendar. When the dates play through my head, I realize the likelihood the result of this test probably won't be what I expected. I've been so consumed with the situation surrounding my aunt and daughter, I hadn't noticed I was not only sick but also late.

Worry overtakes me. I just found out about my daughter, adding an infant seems like more than I can handle. Even my friends know I'm anything but maternal. One of the reasons I gave Carly my cat was because I kept forgetting to feed it. I don't have plants because every plant I've brought into my apartment has shriveled up and died from lack of water. Hell, I have like ten half-used bottles of vitamins because I can't remember to take them every day.

Then there's Casen to think about. He just got a record deal. How fair would it be to throw a baby into the mix? I know how much he wants a family, and as much as he loves music, he would probably give up the deal for a baby. I don't think I could let him do that.

Unsure of everything, I take the test, lay it on the counter, and leave the bathroom before the results appear.

The girls are waiting anxiously for me in the living room. Vivian, as promised, has a cup of Pepto waiting for me. I take it from her, guzzle the chalky substance down, and walk across the room to sit down. Their eyes follow me as I sit in the recliner.

"Well, what did it say?" Carly says, breaking through the silence.

"I don't know, I haven't looked. It's sitting on the counter. I don't think I can look."

Carly and Vivian run to the bathroom, almost knocking each other down in the process. They slowly return with the test, their pale faces and wide eyes are all the confirmation I need.

"Positive, huh?" I say, shell-shocked from my new predicament.

Vivian lays the test on the coffee table, the two pink lines glaring at me…mocking me. The girls take up spots on the couch and loveseat, their shocked expressions matching mine.

"How are you holding up?" Campbell asks, reading my unease.

"What do you mean? This is fantastic!" Carly interjects enthusiastically. "You and Vivian, two babies. How wonderful!"

Campbell offers a me a look of sympathy. We all are aware of Carly's struggles to get pregnant, and now her marital issues. To not only show a lack of enthusiasm but to inform her I'm not sure if I'll be keeping the baby will be like a slap to the face. It will hurt her deeply, but I have to remember this is my situation, not hers.

"Carly, hun, I need to think things through before I make any decisions about this baby."

Her faces scrunches, her disapproval written all over it. "What do you mean, decisions? You would consider not having it?"

"Easy guys," Vivian warns. "This is all a bit of a shock; we shouldn't let our emotions run away with us."

"No," she snaps. "There are people in this world who want nothing more than to have a child but can't, myself included. Yet here you sit with the greatest gift in the world, and you don't want it."

"I didn't say that, Carly," I defend myself. "I just found out I didn't lose my daughter. I need to think about if I can handle all of this on my own. Besides, you've always been the first one to point out how irresponsible I am and what a terrible mother I would be. Shit, you don't even want to send Olivia with me on the camping trip."

"Wait, what do you mean, do it alone, Jen? What about Casen?" Cam inquires. "He's not the type of guy to let you do this by yourself."

I'm under a microscope and the scrutiny is becoming extremely uncomfortable. I stand and move to the window, wishing like hell it would open up and the breeze would carry me away from this conversation.

"Jen, what about Casen?" Vivian presses.

I spin around to the group, my patience wearing, my emotions frayed. "Either way, I'm not telling him."

"What! Why not?" Vivian asks, scooting toward the end of the loveseat.

I sigh and take a seat on the edge of the coffee table, my eyes burning a hole in the beige carpet below my feet. "What kind of person would I be if I told him and put him in a position to choose between the two things he's always wanted?" I look up and focus my attention on the one person I think will understand me the most. "I love him, Campbell. I love him enough to let him go," my voice is a mere whisper as emotion chokes my throat. Losing Casen would feel like suffocating, but I can't take his dream from him either. I know no matter what I say, he would give up music to be with his family.

Campbell slides closer to me and covers my hands with hers. Her voice is soothing, understanding. "Jen, I would never tell you what to do. However, if you love him, don't you think he deserves to know? What kind of person would you be if you took the choice away from him? "

Vivian stands and moves over to the coffee table to sit beside me. "We are here for you, no matter what, doll. We love you," she says, placing her hands on Campbell's which are still resting on mine.

Everyone looks to Carly, who's been silently hanging back since our emotional eruption. Finally, she slides up next to me on the opposite side of Vivian and rests her hands on the pile. "Jen, you are the most loyal, loving person I know. You are stronger than anyone I know. If there was anyone who could handle all of this, it would be you. But don't ever think you would do this alone, we will always be there for you. You need to know, hun, I believe in you…we believe in you."

And just like that, my girls restored my faith in myself. I was going to be a mom, and for once I felt excited about hearing the word.

JEN

What a difference a picture can make. When I had the first sonogram of Abby done, I didn't even look at it. I didn't want to get attached to something I couldn't have. Things are different now. Seeing this baby's image on the screen and holding the image in my hand, all of the indecision I had a few weeks ago has evaporated. All doubts have transformed into butterflies, which are taking up residence in my stomach; I'm overcome with an excitement I've never experienced, and wouldn't trade for anything.

The second I enter my quaint, little apartment, a place I'll have to leave soon if I plan on having two children living with me, I enter the kitchen and stick the ultrasound picture on my refrigerator with my favorite X-rated magnet. My naked man-tini will be the first of many things in this apartment, which will need to go when I childproof my previous life from the space.

A faint knock at the front door draws my attention from the picture of my little jellybean. I still can't believe I already have such an emotional attachment with something which really does look like a jellybean. I told Campbell I would text her after the appointment, but it doesn't surprise me that one of the girls would show up here to hear all about it. There's another knock as I walk across the living room to the door. Unlocking the deadbolt and swinging it open, I'm shocked at who is actually standing on the other side of the doorway.

"Hello, Mother."

I try to examine her appearance as a clue as to what she's doing here. I haven't spoken to her in years, and there is no reason I can think of for her unannounced visit.

I always knew she and my father kept an eye on things to make sure I didn't publicly embarrass them, but nothing I've done recently should have made it back to them as of yet.

Her Chanel pantsuit is freshly pressed and there isn't a hair out of place. Nothing about her appearance looks any different from the last time I saw her, except for one noticeable difference. Her iceberg of a wedding ring is missing. She used to flaunt it as a status symbol…this is who I'm married to and this is what he bought me. Her marriage is all she's ever had. To see her without the ring is alarming.

"I'm sorry to show up like this, I don't have your phone number. Can I come in?" She looks uneasy and nervous that I may close the door on her, and for a moment, I consider just that.

"Sure," I quietly say, moving to the side to allow her entry.

She wanders into the living room, examining my pictures, running her hand along the sofa. Really, she's silently scrutinizing my life, deciding whether she approves of my choices or not. "Your place looks lovely," she finally announces, taking a seat on the chair.

"What are you doing here?" I question before she gets too comfortable.

"I left your father, and I wanted to let you know." I sense her unease with not only saying the words, but embracing her new single life.

I sit down on the couch across the room from her, preparing for the massive explanation, which will be coming my way. My mother was happy to look the other way for many years; I can't imagine what the final straw was which prompted her to leave a life she loved.

"Did something happen?"

"Oh, Jennifer. Too many things have happened. I was too content being oblivious to them. I looked into divorce many times, I just could never find a lawyer who was willing to go up against your father."

"And that's changed?" I ask, still not showing much compassion for the woman who also looked the other way when my father sent me away.

"After his latest extramarital indiscretion with his newest twenty-six year old secretary I searched a little harder and found someone to help me. Once I left, I immediately called your Aunt Maggie to find out about you." Her voice cracks and she covers her mouth, looking away from me.

I grab a tissue from the end table next to me and offer it to her. She accepts and, always the socialite, she delicately dabs her eyes.

"Jennifer, honey, I'm so sorry I didn't believe you, that I didn't stand up for you. I'm not expecting you to forgive me. I honestly don't think I deserve your forgiveness, but I think it's important you hear the words."

"I don't know what to say. It's been a long time."

"Too long. I wish I would have had the courage sooner. I want to be a part of your life, if you'll let me."

I stay silent, unsure how I feel about her presence in my life.

"I don't need an answer right now; I just want to put it on the table. This time, on your terms." She stands up and slides a piece of paper across the coffee table, her phone number written across the card. "When you're ready, if you're ever ready, please call," she says and begins to walk toward the door.

I think of all the relationships that have been damaged, the ones that I've lost. If I have a chance to possibly mend one, I don't want to be the reason it doesn't happen.

"Mom," I murmur, prompting her to stop. "Give me some time, but I'll call."

She turns and smiles at me before walking out the door.

CASEN

Jen has avoided my calls for weeks. I've been busy negotiating contracts with the label, but every available moment I have, I try to get a hold of Jen. Any texts I send are responded to with simple sentences or a single word. I realize I overstepped some boundaries, but I refuse to let her shut me out forever. I figure if I show up at her apartment, she can't avoid me anymore.

My nerves are kicked into overdrive as I climb the stairs to her apartment. I feel my heart beat with each step I take closer to the woman I love. When I finally reach her floor, I pass a well-dressed middle-aged woman in the hallway outside Jen's apartment. Even though Jen's building is a decent one, I can't help but wonder if this lady feels as out of place as she looks. She notices my tattoos and I sense her passing judgment as to the type of guy I am. If I didn't have manners or a pressing mission to attend to, I would do my best to play up the stereotype and make her feel uncomfortable. That's what Jen would do. The woman provides a slight smile as we pass each other, and I smile back at the thought of what my sparkplug would say to this woman.

I finally make it to her door and knock, still unsure of what I'm going to say or how to approach her.

"Mom, I said I would call," she says, opening the door extremely quickly and throwing me off guard. Well, that explains the wealthy woman I saw in the hallway.

"Nope, just me," I tell her with a wave. "You won't answer my calls, you left me no choice."

She nods and moves aside for me to come in, thank God. She leads me to the kitchen and I pull out a barstool at the counter to prepare for the discussion of my life.

As soon as she enters the kitchen, I begin the begging. I need her to forgive the invasion of her privacy. I'm not a groveling man, but the bottom line is, I need this woman.

"I'm sorry for going behind your back, Jen, I didn't want to hurt you. If anything, I wanted to fix something for you," I explain.

"I understand why you did it, Casen," she says, leaning on the counter, her expression giving nothing away as to my fate. "I don't know if I ever would have had the courage to follow through if you hadn't set up the meeting. So in a way, I'm thankful you did what you did."

I must be hallucinating. Never did I think she would be thankful. Pissed, livid, irate…yes, but never thankful. "So where does this leave us then? Are we okay?" I ask, hopeful as to where this conversation is headed.

Instead of answering Jen turns toward the fridge and opens it, hiding her face behind the door. She's avoiding my question. "Do you want something to drink? I'm going to grab a water."

I hop off the barstool and move around the counter to stand behind her. "I don't want a drink, Jen. I want to know if I still have you."

Her shoulders slump in defeat, and I know it's not avoidance. She's hiding something. "You need to focus on the record deal. It's such a great opportunity, I can't let you throw that away for me." Her back is still to me as she stares at the inside of the fridge, which only contains drinks.

Placing my hand on her back, I attempt to soothe her. "I'm not throwing anything way. There's no reason I can't have both." I wrap an arm around her waist and pull her away from the fridge, closing the door once there's room.

That's when I see it. The picture, which steals every bit of air from my lungs. My arm around Jen falls away and my focus on her dissipates. Everything falls away except the little bean of a baby in the photo. My world shifts on its axis and I can hardly catch my breath.

"Please tell me it's mine," I croak out, strangling on each word.

She turns to face me and nods, tears gathering in her eyes. "Casen," she whispers.

"Were you going to tell me? Is that why you've been avoiding me?" I ask, letting the pieces fall into place. I turn and leave the kitchen to give myself some needed space. Jen follows behind me.

"Casen, please. I didn't want you to feel trapped. You love music, I couldn't put you a position where you thought you had to choose one or the other," she pleads as I pace the living room, wearing a hole in the carpet.

"Then don't make me choose," I roar. "Besides, family always comes first. If I needed to choose, it would always be you, whether there were kids involved or not. As much as I love music, I love you more."

"But you're a musician. What would you be if the music wasn't there?" she argues, still not understanding what I'm trying to tell her. I offer my hand and she takes it, allowing my fingers to weave between hers. I lead her to the couch and pull her down to my lap.

"I get to be something way more important than some guy who plays guitar in a band, sparky," I tell her, pushing her hair away from her face and slowly planting soft kisses on both of her cheeks. When she closes her eyes to absorb the feeling of my touch, I lean in and whisper in her ear. "I get to be a dad."

Hoping to find the conviction behind my words, her head pulls back to dive into my eyes, searching them for sincerity. When she finds the love I'm trying to convey, she places her lips to mine in pursuit of reassurance. Her arms tangle around me and peace surrounds us. We are going to be okay. We are going to be a family.

JEN

"I can be there in fifteen minutes," I say before ending the call and throwing my phone into my purse. I knew once the guys found out about the baby, they would want to address the issue somehow. I just figured they would work it out with Casen. So, John's call has me a little flustered.

Slipping on sandals and grabbing my keys, I rush out the door to the pizza place he is supposed to be meeting me at. I haven't ventured into many restaurants in the last few weeks. Whoever gave morning sickness its name is full of shit because it can hit you anytime of the day and I refuse to throw up in public. I'm hoping that pizza is a safe choice.

I make awesome time, for once, and find a front-row parking spot at Beau Jo's Pizza. The smell of sausage and homemade bread filter out of the establishment and attack my senses, but thankfully doesn't spark any waves of queasiness. Swinging open the door, I send up a little prayer that my luck continues and the Hawaiian pizza that I'm about to inhale stays down.

John is standing in the foyer and immediately smiles when he sees me. "Come here, prego," he says as he picks me up and swings me around. "I'm shocked you're on time; I thought we'd be waiting for at least another twenty minutes."

I roll my eyes, at his backwards compliment. He's like a big teddy bear that you can't help but love. I only wish he would get a better handle on the idea of personal space. He constantly invades my bubble and doesn't think twice about it.

"We?" I ask hesitantly when he finally puts me down. "I thought it was just you and I."

John looks at me apologetically but doesn't get the opportunity to answer. The men's room door opens and out walks Royce. "Well, shit. There goes my dinner; the nausea has returned," I say sarcastically.

"Hey, Yoko, glad you could make it," he says with a shit eating grin while he adjusts himself.

I narrow my eyes at John, who instantly looks away from me and walks to our table. So I turn my attention to my nemesis.

"Hello Royce. I noticed you're having a below the belt situation," I say, pointing to his crotch area. "Did Stacy finally give you the clap or is your dick so small, you pissed on your balls?"

I turn on my heel to catch up to John, but Royce moves quickly placing his arm around my shoulder. "Since you're curious, I was shifting things around because my anaconda keeps hitting my knee and I need to move the man snake to the other side before it leaves a mark. I bruise like a peach."

He chuckles at my look of disgust. "You're so gross," I insist as I push him away from me and rush to the table. John pulls my chair out for me, and I sit down as I grab a menu to help avoid any more conversation with Royce.

My plan fails when Royce steals my menu and sits across from me. John looks completely embarrassed but says nothing, so I take the initiative. "What do I owe the pleasure, since we apparently, are not having pizza tonight?"

"We come in peace, Jen," John explains. "Really. We don't mean to piss you off. Right, Royce?" His lips are tight and his eyes narrow, willing Royce to go with the flow. The ostentatious lead singer I know though is not going to give a shit about the request of his friend.

"You bet." Royce affirms as he waves over a waitress. "I don't want to be in the war path of those hormones; a man like me wouldn't survive." John shakes his head and rubs his hands across his face like this discussion is torture for him.

The waitress makes her way to our table, but when she begins to address us, Royce speaks over her. "We don't need to hear the specials, sweetpea. My friend and I will just take whatever you have on tap, but she's knocked up so just bring her a water." He points to me and gives me a little wink which earns him the best crusty look I can throw at him. The waitress looks to me for confirmation, and I just give her a nod that the water is fine. I'm thankful when she leaves without asking anything else.

"So. We wanted to invite you here to find out what your intentions are with are boy?" John probes sheepishly.

"Are you fucking kidding me, guys?" I spit out, annoyed with this dinner outing and Royce's mouth. "This isn't the 1800's and Casen and I aren't in some G-rated courtship. Just ask me what you want to know," I demand impatiently.

"Simmer it down, Madre," Royce interjects. "We know that Casen is in love with you, but we also know he loves his music. We just want to make sure that you have his best interest at heart. That you aren't going to be one of those groupie bitches that snags a man on his way up by getting pregnant, comes between him and his band, and then leaves him when he doesn't have a penny to his name."

"I have been with you guys for a while now, and this is really what you think of me?" I ask unsure if I am more hurt than pissed over their accusation.

"No!" John shouts. "We think you're great. He'll never admit it, but even Royce thinks so. We just want Casen to be happy. He's been through a lot, and he would do anything for anyone, without ever expecting anything in return. We want to know that you'll give as much as you take."

"And that you won't break up the band," Royce interrupts. John elbows him, attempting to shut him up and Royce throws his hands up in defense. "What? We want to know that too."

"Basically, you think I'm going to steal him away from you guys and make him get some shitty nine to five job to support the baby I stuck him with," I clarify.

"No!" John contends.

"Yes," Royce says at the same time.

My face flushes and my body vibrates as the anger takes hold. "You guys are pricks," I snap, as I push my chair away from the table and begin to stand.

"Stop," Royce says grabbing my arm, halting my mad dash out of the building. "Please. We just want to make sure that were on the same page, that's all."

I take a deep breath and slowly return to me seat. "Fine let's hear it."

"We all think you're a kickass chick, Jen," Royce begins.

I tilt my head and narrow my eyes at him, disbelieving his attempt at a compliment.

"We really do," John adds.

"The band is supposed to start recording in a month or so," Royce continues. "Casen has always wanted to be a dad, and he's always wanted to play his music. We need to know that you're going to be okay with how life will change for all of us, that you won't hurt him. He deserves to have both of his dreams come true."

Taking my time to rein in my fury and compose myself, I gather the words that I need to tell these two. "I know what it's like to be in the public eye," I tell them. "There are some great perks, of course, but there is also some fucked up things that come along with fame. None of it is going to scare me away from Casen, guys. I'm here to stay, so you better start treating me like the kickass chick that I am."

Royce cracks a smile. "I can live with that," he says, lightly smacking my back.

"Good. Now buy me a damn Hawaiian pizza."

19

JEN

I must be out of my fucking mind. I take that back, Casen must be out of his fucking mind and I must have had my frontal lobe removed to agree to this camping trip. It's just Casen and me in his little camper with five, I repeat, five children! Blake, the queens of the divas Emma and Grace, Olivia, and Abby who I invited. Hendrix is coming along, but I'm putting him in the adult category so I don't feel so outnumbered. I have to admit, I'm a little worried about my safety. If these kids decide to revolt, it will play out like a scene from *The Hunger Games* and I'm positive my camera isn't going to save my pampered ass.

Casen already went up to the campground and got everything ready for the weekend. Fishing gear, sleeping bags, lawn chairs, and massive amounts of snacks, which could feed a third world country. I don't know how Feed the Children can feed a child on thirty cents a day; our food bill was nowhere near that estimate. My credit card will never be the same.

I'm in charge of picking up the kids and taking them to the campsite. I think everyone is overestimating my managerial skills because I personally don't see this ending well. As I pull into Vivian's driveway, I see all of the kids, aside from Abby who'll be meeting us there, lined up along the entryway. The wide range of moods peering back at me has me shitting myself before I even get out of my car. Blake, as expected, is full of excitement with a perma-grin plastered on his face. The folded arms and frowns, which Emma and Grace are sporting in addition to the mounds of suitcases next to them, suggest they will be the leaders of this weekend's revolution. Then there is little Olivia. I'm not too concerned with her. I've assigned Henri to her for the weekend. I even bought a special leash with clips on both ends so I can connect them together. There will be no wandering off for that little munchkin.

I climb out of the car and I'm immediately met with demands from the rebel leaders.

"Just so you know, we are not okay with this. We will not be touching anything icky and we will report all naughty words back to Daddy," Grace tries to negotiate.

"I'm with you girls, I don't do icky stuff," I respond. "We'll leave that to the boys. Blake, be prepared for a weekend filled with fish guts." Blake perks up even brighter, as do the girls.

"I was beginning to think you changed your mind," Vivian says as she and Carly make their way from the house to meet us. They both wave to Brooks who brings the minivan out of the garage. Yes, the minivan. There are so many kids coming with us we have to borrow Vivian's minivan. Again, I must have had a lobotomy.

Brooks parks the silver beast in front of us and pushes the button to slide open the passenger doors. "Jen, you know I appreciate you doing this so we can have a weekend away, but I'm seriously questioning your sanity. They're my kids, and I have yet to find the courage to take them all on a vacation," he tells me as the kids all throw their bags in and climb into their seats.

"This was Casen's idea. At least you have a drop down DVD player; this is where I'll spend the majority of the weekend."

He hugs and kisses the girls and then buckles them into their seats before making his way to me. "Just bring them back in one piece with as little emotional scarring as possible. I would prefer not to have to explain to their teacher where they learned the colorful language you're known for."

"Hey now, I like to think I use profanity in an appropriate manner which is fucking ladylike." Both of my friends laugh, while Brooks shakes his head.

"There's the Jen we know. Now, don't go getting lost in Walmart," he says, slapping me on the back and heading into the house.

"I hope you bring his cone along," I tell Vivian.

"Are you kidding me, between the baby and the vasectomy, we're looking at months of celibacy. We're using this weekend to our full advantage."

"She's not kidding," Carly adds. "I took her this morning to have the va-jungle tamed."

"Cut me some slack, the belly is getting big enough that I can't reach it myself," Vivian defends herself.

I laugh and give them both a hug and slide into the driver's seat of the ultimate mom wagon. "I'll leave you to your weekend of sex. At least someone will be getting laid. I'd hate my misery to go to waste." Everyone waves good-bye, and I say a small prayer for my survival as we pull out of the driveway.

Between the potty breaks and stops to change out movies, the two-hour drive took three hours. THREE! It's dark as I pull into the campsite, and Casen meets me at the van to carry kids into bed. I make a mental note to tear the van apart in the morning, as somehow Blake lost a shoe. How one loses a shoe in a four by ten confined area, I'll never know, but we won't be doing any exploring until the sneaker is found.

As soon as everyone is settled, Casen and I change into our pajamas, climb into bed, and run through the plan for the following day.

"I thought we would go fishing and hiking. I picked up some water guns for the afternoon when it gets hot," Casen whispers as to not wake the minions.

I snuggle down into the blankets and Henri takes his usual spot wrapped around my legs. "Whatever will pass the hours as quickly as possible. I keep telling myself it's really only one day. Anyone can survive twenty-four hours of something."

He laughs, pulling me into a safe embrace, which has become a feeling of home for me. Kissing my temple and laying a hand on my growing stomach, I melt into him. "I love you, sparkplug. Get some rest; you're going to need it."

It's not the sunlight, which wakes me up, nor is it the smell of bacon and eggs Casen is cooking for everyone. No, I'm woken up to the smack in the face served by a toddler rolling around in my bed. Olivia must have climbed in and fell asleep after Casen woke up to start breakfast. I was not warned of this by Carly. She failed to mention the tossing and turning as well. Now, the first casualty of the trip can be marked down as my right eye.

I free myself from under her arm and tiptoe out of the room. The living area looks like a bomb has exploded. Sleeping bags and pillows are thrown everywhere, body parts poke out from various pieces of the bedding. While I'm not sure where to walk to not step on anyone, I'm thankful they are asleep. Well, they are asleep until Casen starts jingling a damn triangle like we're on a cattle drive. "Come and get it," he hollers. Everyone pops up, wide-eyed and freaked out.

"Have you never heard the phrases, don't poke the bear and never wake a sleeping baby?" I ask Casen when he walks in the door. I bite my lip trying to rein in the colorful language Brooks mentioned. "Momma bear," I say pointing to myself. "Sleeping babies," I add, waving my hands over the kids spread out on the floor.

"Sorry guys, breakfast is ready. We have to get moving while the fish are still biting." Then he closes the camper door and the kids fall back onto their pillows.

"Come on, guys. If we don't get up, he'll be back with that jingling thing again." My advice is met with groans. Blake even throws his pillow at me. "If you wait too long, he'll feed all of the food to Henri," I add, moving over everyone and opening the camper door to go outside. That gets their attention and they begin moving around as I close the door to fill my own plate to start the day.

Thankfully, my morning sickness has passed for the most part and has been replaced by a massive-sized appetite, so when Casen hands me a plate I attack it like a starving person. I'm not at all bashful about the food I may have smeared all over my face because of my slacking table manners. I notice Casen staring at me intently, probably wondering how much food I can actually eat or get on my face.

"In my book, pregnancy gives me a free pass on the use of napkins," I tell him, digging in for more.

"I said nothing, sparky," he says in surrender with a laugh.

"Yeah, I know what you're thinking," I respond between mouthfuls.

Within the hour we manage to get everyone fed, cleaned up, and loaded for fishing. Abby shows up just in time to head to the lake. Nervous doesn't even begin to describe what I'm feeling about her being a part of this weekend. I want her to have fun, I want her to like me, and I don't want to forget to feed her like I did with the cat. I'm glad our first weekend together will include the other kids to serve as a buffer.

I gather the girls and we select the prime fishing spot while the boys unload the fishing gear and cooler filled with drinks and snacks. Trudging through the grass the quarter mile hike to the lake, I think I heard every excuse possible as to why Emma and Grace could no longer continue. Bugs, poison ivy, snakes—which I banned all further discussion about—dirt on their purses, I heard it all.

"We're here, girls!" I happily announce when we finally arrive at the fishing spot. "Now do you remember what I told you about the bait?" I ask them as we begin to set up chairs.

"No worms, ask for the good stuff," Emma repeats from the pep talk I gave during breakfast. I informed them how Casen would try and make them fish with worms, but if they wanted to get a good fish they need to use salmon eggs. I fully intend on coming out ahead on this fishing trip.

The boys join us and begin running the lines on the poles. "What kind of bait does everyone want?" Casen asks and looks to the girls to back up his plan for victory.

"I want to use the worms!" Blake shouts excitedly. I don't really think he cares if he catches fish, Blake would be happy playing in the wiggly worms. I shake my head at his naivety. Casen lets him stick his hand in the plastic container and his face lights up at the sensation of the worms on his skin. As soon as his worm in on the hook and cast into the water, he moves on to the next pole.

Abby gives me a look of confidence and requests Power bait for her red fishing pole. She takes a seat in a lawn chair and begins practicing casting and reeling it in, over and over again instead of letting the line sit in the water.

Olivia isn't the slightest bit interested in fishing and has focused her energy on the butterflies in the grass behind us. Thank goodness for the dual leash invention I've attached to her and Hendrix. As long as she doesn't eat any of the bugs, we should be good to go.

Emma and Grace have a different plan in mind. I give them a look and a nod when Casen asks about their lines. "We want the good the stuff," Emma announces, looking to Grace. They grab their fluffy purses and open them with a devilish smile. "We brought scrambled eggs."

"We're going to catch the biggest fish, huh, Jen?" Grace adds as they each pull out handfuls of their breakfast leftovers. Apparently, we had a breakdown in communication or at least a mistranslation.

"You plan on fishing with scrambled eggs, girls? I've never heard of that," Casen inquires as he puts together his own line.

"Jen said you would try and make us use worms, but we aren't falling for it," Grace explains with her clean hand securely on her hip to emphasize her point.

"Yeah, we're going to help Jen win!" Emma says, throwing her hand in the air and then looking for a high-five from me. Playing the middle ground, I give her a gentle tap in the middle of her palm as a reluctant, half-assed high-five. I figure it still counts.

"Oh, really?" Blake interrupts.

"Um, yeah," Grace responds, throwing as much attitude as her little voice and body can put together.

"How about the loser has to make lunch?" Casen says. "You guys and your scrambled eggs versus us boys and our worms."

I look back and forth, unsure how to proceed. If we were using salmon eggs against his worms I would totally take the bet, but freakin' scrambled eggs? Those girls are killing me. If I end up having to cook lunch, our trip may get cut short because of food poisoning. There is no sense in pretending I can cook anything except popcorn; and let's face it, even that isn't a sure thing.

Before I can give my opinion on the bet, the girls are jumping up to shake Casen's hand to accept the challenge. They rush to me and help load up their lines. I pack them as best I can with their eggs and launch their lines into the lake.

"Oh my God! My line is moving," Abby shouts just as I get everyone settled. She's jumping up and down, waving her hands around, unsure of what to do with the bobbling pole. I grab it from where it's wedged on her chair and hand it to her.

"Start reeling it in, hun," I tell her, helping her to hold the rod. Skipping along the top of the water as the line is brought in, her fish is gorgeous. Huge and slippery, we struggle to get it off the hook and onto the cord we have set up to store the fish we catch, but we accomplish it with gigantic smiles on our faces.

Just as we finish loading up Abby's line with bait again, our Barbie and Hello Kitty poles baited with scrambled eggs begin to wobble. "We got one, too!" the girls scream.

"Um, since your pole isn't really doing much, you think you could help for a second?" I ask Casen triumphantly. Surprisingly he hops up and helps Emma with her line.

"Wow, girls, I think you might be on to something," he says as uses the net to capture Emma's fish, which is the size of a whale.

The girls couldn't lose; they would throw out their lines and immediately reel them back in. It isn't long before Blake makes his way to our area begging for scrambled eggs. Thankfully, the girls take pity on him and share their eggs. Soon he, too, catches a fish.

By the time we're done, there is no question who won our battle of the sexes challenge. At camp, everyone enjoys the fish Blake and Casen prepare and the girls are even decent sports about winning, rarely throwing their victory in the boys' faces.

By mid-afternoon the heat of day has us sweating to death and we veto the hiking idea, opting instead for the water gun fight.

"Kids versus adults," Blake suggests. "We'll even let you have Henri," he adds to sell his idea. The kids all cheer and we have no option but to agree to the teams.

"Our only stipulation is you stay in our camp area and you have to keep Olivia with you at all times so she doesn't wander off," I declare.

"Agreed," Blake and Abby both say. "We need time to prepare, though," Blake adds.

We nod and hand over a pile of water guns, which are already filled, and a bucket to fill with water to refill their guns. Everyone separates and prepares for the water war of the century.

Casen and I work together to fill our guns and devise a plan to pick off each kid, one at a time. Grabbing our rubber bucket, loading our pants with water pistols, and holding super soaker Nerf guns, we exit the camper ready for battle.

Our competition has been hard at work as well. Each kid is decorated in war paint, either with mud or makeup. The minions are all armed and ready to take us out.

"Ready! Set! Go!" Casen shouts, prompting everyone to scream and run toward each other firing their weapons in a steady stream of water. Judging from the soaked status of everyone involved, I'm not seeing how there can be a clear winner, but we're having fun so it makes no difference.

One-by-one, we each surrender when we run out of water. When it's all over we each find a place in the sunshine and lie out to dry off. With Abby on one side of me and Olivia on the other, I relax and enjoy the moment. That is until my nose senses something vile. No, vile isn't a strong enough word, pungently horrendous might do a better job.

I follow my nose and it directs me to our little Olivia. I take a deep whiff and instantly pull away. Poop, she smells like human shit. Turning to the group, I begin my interrogation. "Guys, what did you use for your war paint?"

"We used mud," Blake answers, pointing to himself and Abby.

I look to Grace and she immediately shakes her head. "No way, mud is gross. Emma and I used our makeup."

I look to Casen, and he looks as confused as I feel. "Who painted Olivia?" I ask. Everyone looks around shaking their heads. No one fesses up to painting her, so I go to the source. "Olivia, how did you get your war paint?"

"Me painted," she says, pointing to the stripes running up and down her arms and on her cheeks.

"Very nice, baby. What did you use to paint?"

"Poop!" she shouts with a smile. "Me made poopy paint."

My compassionate smile fades into a look of disgust. I slowly turn to Casen as my dry heaves begin. "I can't. You have to deal, Casen," I whisper in-between heaves. "I just can't do poop."

"To the camper everyone, let's cleanup for dinner and s'mores," he laughs. I follow behind as all the kids head to the camper, Olivia with an enormous smile of pride on her face from her handiwork. "Poop, the kid painted herself with poop," I whisper to myself in disbelief as we head to the bathroom to wash the war paint away.

The cars are packed, and we make it back to Vivian's house in record time. More than likely it's because they slept the whole way home, thus no potty breaks. The entire drive home, I replay the weekend over and over in my head and think about how surprisingly well Casen and I handled it.

Feeling relatively proud of my parenting experience and even happier about spending the weekend with Abby, I pull into Vivian and Brooks' driveway, content with how things went, yet ready to hand over the keys to the mom van.

I turn off the ignition and turn in my seat to face the kids who've begun to wake up. "Rise and shine, everyone. Review time. What are we going to share with your moms and dads?"

"We caught big fish and ate lots of s'mores," they repeat in unison.

"And what do we not talk about because it never happened?" I continue.

"Poopy paint," they all respond.

I whip back around in my seat and hit the button to open the doors. "Nice job, crew. Thank you for using Jen's mobile service. You may now vacate the van, using the nearest exit."

Fuck yeah, I have this mom shit in the bag.

20

JEN

I never got the chance to do the nesting thing the first time around, and this time, Casen has prepared enough for both of us. It's 3 a.m., only a week from my due date, and of course I'm up for yet another bathroom break. Casen is asleep, enjoying a solid night's rest. I don't remember what eight hours of sleep is like, but I'm positive I was a much friendlier person then. Quietly tiptoeing down the hallway, I stop outside the nursery to peek in on all that Casen has done already for our little guy.

Pushing the door open, I pick up a stuffed animal from his crib and sit down in the rocking chair we found at an antique store. The nursery is primed in superhero décor, which Casen has assured me will yield us a miniature dark knight and not a Howard Walowitz. I caved and now there are giant Captain America and Batman canvases hanging above his bed instead of footballs or sailboats.

Running my fingers through the fur of the teddy bear, my mind wanders to the last time I was days away from having a baby. The dread of having to give her away, the shame, the sadness; I didn't want that day to ever arrive. I'm thankful for my aunt's deception, because it has given me a second chance to correct that wrong…make Abby a part of my life instead of a memory of my past.

Now here I am, on the verge of having another child, a child I didn't think I deserved to have. For the first time in a long time I'm excited for what the future holds, not just for me, but for the family I now have.

"Everything okay, sparky?" Casen whispers, leaning on the doorframe. He is absolutely scrumptious with his brown hair in disarray, and dark grey sweats hanging off his sculpted hips. It's a shame I can't even reach my own ass to wipe it, or I might act on the urge. I'm bendy, but maneuvering around this belly would require Cirque du Soleil training.

I smile at the thought of our sex life returning to active status…six weeks from now. "Yup, I'm good," I murmur back as I continue rocking. "I can't believe in less than a week, this room will have our baby in it and then Abby will be moving in."

"It feels surreal, huh?"

"Are you sure you're all right with everything?" I ask. I know I shouldn't worry, but there are times I'm afraid Casen will feel overwhelmed and want to walk away. I know it's my own insecurities, but every once in a while they creep into my mind.

Casen enters the nursery and kneels at my feet, grabbing my hands. "Jen, I love you more than I thought it could be possible to love someone. I love you, not only because of who you are, but because of what you have given me…a family. I could never be anything but grateful."

It's exactly what I needed to hear to calm my rising anxiety. He kisses my expanding belly and stands. "Come on, love, let's go back to bed," he says, offering me his hand like he has a million times over the last nine months. Just like I have a million times before, I slide my hand in his.

CASEN

I feel a sharp nudge in the middle of my back, rousing me from a deep sleep. Looking to the clock on the nightstand the bright green numbers read 4 a.m. *You have got to be fucking kidding me. We've only been back to bed for an hour and Jen decides to practice her nightly ninja skills*, I think to myself as I attempt to fall back to sleep. Sharing a bed is not something she's adapted well to, the concept of his and her sides of the bed is a lost concept in this house. She thrashes around in her sleep so much that snuggling or spooning is actually code for restraining her from karate chopping my nut sack in her sleep. It's not even that she's having nightmares; she's just a wild sleeper.

Closing my eyes, I feel the deep calm of sleep begin to take hold once again when a solid push nails me. "Casen, wake up," Jen says with another nudge. Only one eye pops open, I'll reserve the second once I find out the reason for this early morning wake-up call.

"We are out of watermelon and ice-cream. I'll get more tomorrow, just let the sun come up first," I tell her, snuggling back into the blankets and closing my eyes.

"No, Casen, wake up. I think my water broke," she says in a surprisingly calm, hushed tone.

Both eyes snap open and I rise up in bed as quickly as possible, getting tangled in the sheet and nearly falling out of bed. "What? Are you sure," I ask, flipping on the lamp but remaining quiet as not to wake Hendrix.

"Well, I'm not positive, but I'm having a fluid situation and I'm pretty sure I know how not to piss myself," she says sarcastically, her volume indicating her lack of concern for keeping Henry asleep.

I jump out of bed and run to my shirt and shoes. I grab all of the bags we've had packed for weeks and stand waiting for direction. "Are you having contractions? Are you in pain? Do we need to leave for the hospital? Why aren't you getting dressed?" I fire off question after

161

question in lightning speed, unable to contain my nerves and excitement.

"I'm not, that's why I'm not sure if my water broke. I would think I would already be in pain if it had."

"Well, what did the book say?" We bought every baby preparation book available, surely something in one of them mentions this scenario.

"I didn't read them. I got to week twenty-four and then started skimming and looking at pictures. I've given birth before; I figured I didn't really need to read up on that part. How does one not know they are in labor?" I nearly drop the bags as a now wide-awake Henri barrels me over, wanting to go outside.

"Well, let's go just to be safe. Worst case scenario, they send us home." I leave the room with the bags to let the dog out and load the car. Hustling back into the bedroom after buckling in the infant seat, I find Jen doubled over breathing deeply.

"You okay, sparkplug?" I ask tentatively.

"What in the hell have you been doing? I'm definitely in labor, we need to get to the hospital," she squeezes out each word through clenched teeth and my stomach begins to twist in knots at the sight of the woman I love in such pain. I know I need to snap into action, but panic mode has set in and I stand there frozen at the realization I'm about to be a father.

Her contraction subsides and she storms over to me, snatching the car keys from my hand. "I'm headed to the hospital; if you want a ride, I suggest you get your ass in gear." That's all I need to get me moving.

"I'm focused. Give me the keys, I'll get you there," I yell after her as she reaches for the driver's door to our new SUV. Of course, Nelly is tucked safely in the garage, we sold off Jen's car and bought this a month ago. I run around to the passenger side, lay a towel on the fresh leather, and ease her into the seat.

Throwing the car into drive, I race down the street of our suburb, away from our new home we bought after signing the record deal, and toward my new family. Jen's eyes are closed, her brows scrunched, breathing deeply with each painful contraction. I notice my breathing matches hers, my brows scrunch together when hers do. I only wish I could also take some of her pain away.

"Sparky, you hanging in there?" I ask, bracing myself for a harsh, abrasive response.

"Mmm hmm," she mumbles through a deep cleansing breath. She briefly opens her eyes to see we're stopped at a red light. Unfortunately for me, we're the only car in a two-mile radius. "You only have one job, Casen. Get me to the hospital," she snaps. "Is it really imperative that we stop at this light at 4 a.m. when there are no other cars around? Treat it like a four-way stop, dammit," she hollers as the pain of the next contraction takes hold.

"Okay, babe. I'm hurrying. We're only five more minutes away from the hospital, just hang in there." I try to keep my voice as calm as possible as I slam the gas pedal to the floor and barrel through the light.

I cut those five minutes to three by disregarding all traffic rules, pulling the car into a parking space just shy of 4:30. I rush around the car to grab Jen's bag and help her out of the car. Our pace drastically slows though, as she has to stop to breathe through each contraction, which by my mental count are only two minutes apart. It probably takes us more time to walk to the labor and delivery nurses' station than it did for me to drive us here. I will not be mentioning that to Jen, though. I would like to have more children in the future and I've learned she's keen on collecting the man parts of men who piss her off.

"Can I help you?" a plump, middle-aged woman behind the desk asks, obviously irritated she's working the night shift. Pam, the desk worker, immediately rubs me the wrong way, and I begin to silently pray our interaction with this woman ends after we leave the check-in counter.

"My girlfriend is in labor. Her water broke about thirty minutes ago," I tell her, doing my best to be polite as Jen concentrates on her current contraction.

"Are you sure your water broke?" she asks dismissively.

Jen looks up from the white tile floor which has become the all-important focal point and serves me the iciest of death glares. Instead of relaying the message that she is seconds away from being stabbed in the eye with her flower pen, I opt for, "We're pretty sure."

"Okay, well, have you filled out any of the pre-admission paperwork?"

"No, our appointment is next week."

When she rolls her eyes and heads off to another room to retrieve the paperwork, all of my patience disintegrates. "Are you fucking kidding me?" I spit out in a hushed tone. Jen shushes me, but I ignore her. "What are they going to do, send us to the parking lot to deliver the baby in the car?"

Jen twirls around, pinning me with the death glare previously reserved for Pam. "You will shush, Casen Thompson. These women have to put their hands near my vagina; you will not piss them off."

Stepping into the fray of growing tension, Pam returns with the necessary paperwork along with another nurse. "Here, you're going to have to fill this out," she says, shoving a clipboard at me.

"You can follow me to an observation room," nurse number two says.

"Observation room? Do you think she's not in labor?" I ask.

"Well, sir, we have to be sure before we send you to delivery," Pam chimes in.

We're taken to a room the size of my closet with a single bed and a monitor. Jen changes into a hospital gown and climbs into the bed so the nurse can attach the monitor. Instantly the baby's heartbeat echoes through the room and the screen shows the peaks and valleys of Jen's contractions.

"How are we coming with the paperwork?" Pam asks.

"I just got in the room, it's not done yet."

"I'll be back in a few minutes to get it from you," she says before leaving the room. I give her a little salute to send her off.

I'm not sure what observation is taking place because as soon as the monitor is connected, nurse two leaves as well and we're left alone for the next thirty minutes.

"You need to get someone; these are getting bad," Jen breathes through a contraction. I jump into action, thankfully though, nurse number two walks through the door, so I don't have to track anyone down.

"Let's go ahead and see how things are progressing," she says, taking the monitor strips in her hand to examine them. "Looks like you've been having good ones."

I grind my teeth at the lack of care or concern anyone is showing us. I know this is no big deal to these two women who see deliveries all day every day, but this is scary and exciting for me and I have no idea what to expect.

"I have to push," Jen shouts, gaining everyone's attention. My freak-out mode is now soaring, but nurse number two still sees no reason for alarm; never mind we're still in a damn observation room.

"Let's check things out, hun, just keep breathing," she says as she places gloves on and prepares for what has to be one of the most uncomfortable things I've ever seen. All I can think is, *I wonder if this is how Five Finger Death Punch got its name.*

The nurse's eyes bug out and she jumps from the bed, shouting into the hall. "Call delivery, I need some help in here."

"What's going on, where are we going?" I ask, grabbing the bags as several nurses storm into the room and begin wheeling the bed into the hallway. There's no time for IVs or an epidural. Jen's going to be pissed she didn't get to wear her designer hospital gown. She waited weeks for that thing to be delivered because she thinks hospital issued ones are ugly and no matter how hard you try, your ass always hangs out the back.

"Everything is okay, we need to get her to a delivery room, the baby is here," a nurse reassures me. I'm following close behind the hoard of people until I see good old Pam waiting for me with her clipboard. "Sir, you missed a signature, can you please follow me to finish the paperwork?"

My. Head. Explodes. With Jen out of earshot, I feel it's safe to unleash the verbal diarrhea I've wanted to spill onto this woman since I got off the elevator.

"With all due respect, you can shove that clipboard up your ass. I understand this paperwork is important, but making sure my girlfriend and baby are safe sits a little higher for me. Maybe if you had worried a little less about those forms and a little more about the patient, my baby would be born in a delivery room with an actual doctor instead of the fucking hallway for everyone to see." I swipe the clipboard from her hand, sign the missing piece, and toss it back to her. "I don't want to see your face again while we are here."

I turn and race down the hall, following the sound of chaos to a room mid-way down the corridor. I quickly get to Jen's side and wipe the sweat from her face. "He's almost here," I whisper in her ear.

The on-call doctor barely enters the room in time to catch the baby. There's no delivering about it, she might as well have had a catcher's mitt.

I cut the cord and when I hear him cry all of the drama and frustration to get to this moment fades away. Thankful, I'm just thankful. Looking down at Jen, worn out and shaking from the drop in adrenaline, I can't hide my grin. "Good job, sparkplug," I say, leaning in to kiss her forehead. "He's perfect, you did so well. I love you, Jen. Thank you for giving me a family."

"I love you too," she smiles. "Go. Go check on Ryker," she murmurs, barely able to keep her eyes open.

Excited but nervous, I tentatively approach the baby warmer where the nurses are taking care of Ryker. "Hi, little man," I coo, allowing his tiny hand to grasp my index finger. "You were in a bit of a rush."

"He's fine, sir, but we're going to need to take him to the nursery to suction him out better and give him a little oxygen," a nurse interrupts.

Before I can question her or ask if I'm allowed to go with him, buzzers and alarms ring out around Jen's bed. When I see she's unconscious, I rush to her and grab her lifeless hand.

"Jen!" I shout, shaking her. "Sparkplug, wake up." There's no response. My frozen panic sets in as the pandemonium of the room swarms around me, pushing me away from Jen's bedside.

"Start an IV!"

"Push the epinephrine!"

"She's bleeding out, get the O.R. and anesthesiologist prepped!"

"Someone get her chart, now!"

"Sir..."

"Sir…"

"Sir?"

"I'm sorry," I whisper, snapping out of my trapped state of anxiety.

"Sir, does she have any known allergies or any history of clotting disorders?" the nurse asks me.

"No. She's healthy. There haven't been any issues with the pregnancy," I tell her and she quickly turns, leaving me standing alone once again. "What's going on, is she going to be okay?" I ask. No one answers; everyone is too busy working on Jen.

I push my way through the crowd to get near Jen, and grab her hand once again. "Please, what's going on? Is she going to be okay?" I yell to the crowd, my voice breaking with the strain of the tears I'm holding back.

"Her blood pressure is crashing again!" a nurse yells and pushes me out of the way.

As nurses pass by me, I try to get their attention to get information, but no one notices me as they stay focused on feverishly working on Jen.

"Someone please tell me what's happening!" I shout as loudly as possible. Everyone stops working for a moment to look at me. "Get him out of here," the doctor says, drawing my attention to the space in which she's working. Blood is covering the floor, more blood than I've ever seen. I can read the concern on the doctor's face, and I know in that moment, I could lose her.

More beeping grabs everyone's attention. "Get the crash cart!" the doctor yells as two nurses attempt to escort me from the room.

"Please. Please, let me stay. I can't let her be alone. I need to be with her." I fight to get back in the room as the crash cart is wheeled in.

"Sir, we are doing the best we can to help her. You need to stay out and let us do that. If we get her stabilized, we will let you know," she says before rushing back into the room.

Moments later a team of nurses and the doctor wheel Jen's bed out of the room and run down the hallway toward the operating room. I watch stunned as the love of my life, my sparkplug, floats away from me. I look at the nurse who took me into the hallway, the one who attempted to reassure me. I replay her words in my mind, but only one sticks out and I stumble on it like a crack in the pavement, a wrinkle in my world.

"If," I whisper, sliding down the wall and letting my suppressed emotions of the moment pour out of me.

VIVIAN

I hear the car honk and I kiss Brooks one last time good-bye. "I'll call you when I know more," I tell him. He nods and continues to rock our baby daughter, Joslyn, back to sleep.

Hustling down the stairs and out the entryway, I find two of my best friends in the car waiting for me.

"Hustle, Viv, we have to get all the way across town," Carly says from the passenger seat as I climb into the back.

"Don't worry, I'll get us there," Campbell interjects after I close my car door. Gravel kicks up from under our wheels as she peels out of the driveway. Surprisingly there is a lack of conversation in the car as we make the thirty minute trek across town to the hospital. There's a nervous tension in the car with hope, concern, and anxiety all mixed together in a thick ball of emotion a person could choke on.

"Has anyone heard from Casen?" I ask.

Campbell's eyes meet mine in the rearview mirror. "Not since I called you," she says, before directing her attention back to the road. I settle into the leather seats and watch the street lamps and lonely cars pass by as we race across the city. There are towns, which never sleep, but looking at the streets of Denver, we are a people who apparently need their rest; it's desolate outside. Right now, though, I wouldn't complain about that, it helps us to get to the hospital faster.

Piling out of the car, we follow the signs to the labor and delivery section of the hospital. Once the door is unlocked for us and we're allowed through security, the three of us rush through the double doors. We only make it a few steps into the main hallway before we see Casen sitting on the ground outside a delivery room.

We all halt and my heart sinks…we're too late.

"Casen?" Campbell says apprehensively, trying to get his attention. He looks up, his eyes bloodshot and streaks of dried tears scattered down his cheeks. "Where are they?" she asks.

His face scrunches in pain before he looks back down at the ground. He takes a deep breath before looking at us once again to respond. He then says the two words I never thought I would hear, and will never forget.

"They're gone."

21

CASEN

"I wish your momma could be here, little guy," I tell Ryker before kissing his head. He giggles and wiggles in my arms, and I'm grateful he's been quiet during the ceremony and he hasn't thrown up on my suit.

"Um, Dad?" A word I haven't quite haven't gotten used to, but I don't get tired of hearing.

"Yes, sweetheart, what's up?" I ask Abby.

"Blake and the girls are over there by the snacks, can I go hang out with them?" her voice meek and unsure. We're still maneuvering through our new relationship, but we're doing well. It's an adjustment for everyone, but I'm glad Abby has decided to live with us full-time.

"Absolutely. Stay with the group and don't leave the building. Deal?"

"Deal." She leans down and lands a kiss on Ryker's cheek and takes off toward the kids. It still amazes me how much she looks like her mother. She's a petite little thing with the same wavy blonde hair, which she insists on having up off her neck. She prefers jeans and T-shirts to dresses and ribbons which makes life super easy on me.

Vivian's kids have completely accepted her and included her in their world, which I'm thankful for. These people have become more than friends, they are my family…the family I've always wanted.

Vivian bounces down the aisle, her eyes scanning the rows, more than likely looking for her children. When her eyes land on me, she offers a gentle smile.

"They're over at the snack table," I tell her while standing to give her a hug, her usual greeting.

"Thank you. I should have guessed. They wandered away from their seat after my speech," she says, directing her line of sight to the snacks and waving at the kids. "How are you guys?" she asks, taking Ryker's hand and playing with his fingers.

"Things are good. You know Jen would have liked to have been here," I offer.

"Oh, Casen, I know," she smiles. "It means a lot that you and the kids are here. We've been working on opening this at-risk youth foundation for almost a year; I'm happy to see it finally come to fruition. I think this was the perfect way to honor my dad's memory."

I look around the room, the main banquet room for the foundation, which will be used for events to raise more money to keep the foundation going. It's decorated elegantly; the whole building was put together well. I would expect nothing less from Brooks and Vivian. "Everything looks fantastic, Viv. You guys should be proud of what you're accomplishing here. I wish something like this was available when I was a kid."

"Thank you, Casen that means a lot." Her eyes look past me and a huge grin breaks across her face. "I can't believe she made it."

I turn around toward the entrance to look at who's caught Vivian's attention. The second I see her, I find a smile, which matches Vivian's. When Jen sees us, she rushes down the rows and throws her arms around Ryker and me. "Everything is done," she whispers. "We're legally a family now."

She then turns to Vivian and bear hugs her as well. "I am so proud of you, Viv. I wouldn't have missed this for the world," she says, her voice breaking with emotion.

"Thank you, Jen. How are you even here? I didn't think you would make it," Vivian asks, breaking away from the embrace.

"Preston didn't protest anything, he signed over all rights. My aunt was there to sign all the necessary paperwork. It's done, Abby is legally ours," she sighs with a smile.

This has been a long road, one that led both her and Abby to counseling to come to grips with the past and their current relationship. After paternity tests were completed and it was established that Preston was in fact Abby's father, we petitioned to have his paternity rights revoked. Thankfully, it didn't require a legal fight, since he willingly signed whatever was needed to silence what he had done to Jen. The statute of limitations on the rape expired, but the courtroom of public opinion can be just as brutal; Preston is smart enough to know that.

"Did your mother show up?" I inquire. I'm not sure whether now is the time to address it or not, but I can't help but ask. Her mother and this court hearing have been weighing on her. Since Jen's parent's divorce was finalized, the two have slowly been working on rebuilding their relationship, but this hearing was like facing all of those demons again for her.

Jen's eyes cast down to the floor. Immediately, I reach out and grasp her hand to give it a gentle, reassuring squeeze. My touch draws her attention back to me and her eyes meet mine.

"I didn't invite her. I just couldn't," she explains. "I asked her to go to dinner with us tomorrow to celebrate, but I just couldn't have her there. It would have been too much."

Seeing the emotion build in her eyes, I pull her close and wrap my arm her. "It's alright, sparky. You don't have to explain," I murmur. Jen nods into my chest and relaxes into me. Our moment is short lived though, as Ryker begins to whine from being smashed between us.

"Sorry little man," Jen chuckles as we pull away from one another. "I'm going to go let Abby know," she adds, kissing me and Ryker before running over to the kids and gathering Abby in her arms.

It's hard to believe a few months ago I almost lost her. When they wheeled her away to the operating room, I thought it was over. Seeing her open her eyes after surgery in the recovery room gave me a relief I don't think I'll ever find a comparison for. It was the worst and best day of my life.

Noticing Jen's departure from the conversation, Carly and Campbell hustle to mine and Vivian's side.

"Give me that baby," Carly says, taking Ryker from my arms and snuggling him against her shoulder. "Ah, I love that smell," she adds, inhaling deeply.

"What? Has he pooped?" I ask.

"No," she laughs. "Baby smell. I think you need to let me babysit more often."

"Anytime."

"Enough baby talk, she'll be back any minute. Let me see it," Campbell interrupts.

"Did Lakin get the camper all ready for us?" I ask her.

"Everything is good to go," she answers quickly. "We got back this morning."

"We?" I question, but she ignores me and gestures to move it along.

I grab the diaper bag and unzip the inside pocket where I had stashed the ring. I knew the girls would want to put their seal of approval on it, so I brought it just in case. The three of them circle around me to shield any viewing eyes.

"Really? The diaper bag?" Vivian asks disapprovingly.

"What? It's the one place Jen wouldn't look," I explain. "I love her, but when is the last time she changed a diaper? Seriously, girls."

They giggle and agree, but once again Campbell pushes us along by grabbing the black velvet box from my hand and snapping it open. The shimmer from the diamond prompts them all to sharply inhale.

Vivian and Campbell both squeal.

"Gorgeous."

"It really is, good job, Casen."

"It's yellow," Carly says confused. "You know it's supposed to be an engagement ring, right?"

"It's a canary diamond…the color of dandelions," I explain.

"I don't get it," she says.

I take the ring from Campbell and run my fingers around the yellow stone and the two white diamonds, which sit on either side, signifying our children. Looking across the room, I find Jen looking right back at me. Her playful smile makes me smile as well, our love silently being expressed. She is what I've been waiting for…the weed amongst the flowers, the dandelion amongst the roses.

My eyes follow her as she moves in our direction. "Don't worry, girls," I say keeping my eyes glued to my future bride. "She'll understand."

The End

LOOK FOR CAMPBELL AND CARLY'S STORIES EARLY 2015.